SIDE EFFECTS

SIDE EFFECTS

JEFF MENAPACE

MIND MESS PRESS

2018

CHAPTER 1

Upstate Pennsylvania
After midnight

Deep in the woods, the man at his feet, cuffed and gagged, started crying.

Crying.

God, he loved it when they broke like that.

And oh, how he wanted to giggle and taunt this one—number six—just like he'd done all the others.

Instead, he resisted.

Yes, for this one he decided to keep his cool. He was becoming a professional, after all. Giggling and taunting felt wrong tonight. Amateurish. He would be giggling on the inside, of course—elated and downright giddy on the inside—but how much more terrifying for this one to see him calm and collected as he busied himself preparing the ritual that had become his life's work?

Far more terrifying—or so he hoped.

Whether he was becoming a professional or not, each new one *was* a learning experience. Only arrogant fools felt there was a ceiling. He knew that true growth had no ego, had no ceiling. Knew that if he allowed himself to perceive each new one as yet another step on a staircase leading him towards unparalleled greatness, well, then—and he snickered silently to himself at the tired old cliché—the sky truly was the limit.

And if it wasn't? If keeping cool *didn't* feel as rewarding as the others? If taunting and capering about with a lunatic's grin proved to be more fulfilling after all? Well, he would simply use that experience as another step to be added to his staircase, happily climbed for next time.

Because there *would* be a next time. And a time after that. And then one after, and so on.

The thought of such a promising future almost broke his cool. A titter nearly escaped. He hid it as a cough and resumed preparation of his ritual while the man at his feet continued sobbing through his gag, futilely struggling against the cuffs binding his wrists behind his back.

"Nearly time," he said to number six, spiking the shovel into the sizable mound of dirt next to the freshly dug grave. "Nearly time, indeed. Just got to check a few more things, and then it will be showtime, good sir." And then he *did* break his cool, his own wit the culprit. He succumbed to a snicker and felt his bladder threaten to empty with excitement. He coughed again to conceal his delight, then pinched the tip of his penis to warn his bladder.

.   .   .

Time to begin. Time for number six to become part of his new life's work. The anticipation was excruciating; keeping his cool was becoming harder and harder. Downright maddening. Oh Christ, why fight it? Once he began the show, number six would be horrified beyond all measure; keeping his cool wasn't going to add any additional horror to that. Why, number six probably wouldn't even notice, he'd be so busy touring hell.

Touring hell. That was a good one.

So then let it out and enjoy!

And he would have…had he not heard voices in the distance.

The sound that escaped his mouth now was anything but joyous. It was a soft, defeated cry, the incredulous little gasp of a man who'd bet it all on a seemingly unbeatable hand, only to find that *seemingly* had been the operative word.

Number six apparently heard the voices in the distance growing closer too. His eyes widened with desperate hope, his sobs into his gag now muffled cries for help.

Devastated, he snatched the shovel from the mound of dirt and brought it down onto number six's head once, twice, and then a final time to ensure he was quite dead. He then kicked the body of number six—though he supposed he could no longer refer to him as number six now, dammit—into the freshly dug grave, quickly gathered his things, and hurried away with a disappointment in his heart that was almost crippling.

CHAPTER 2

Philadelphia, Pennsylvania

Dr. Cole opened his notebook and clicked a pen. "Whenever you're ready, Maggie."

I asked: "You know what today is, Dr. Cole?"

"No."

"It's Irony Appreciation Day."

Dr. Cole gave an amused little smile. "Is it?"

I nodded. "It is. Do you appreciate irony?"

"Depends on the circumstances, I suppose."

I raised an index finger. "Ah, but it's Irony *Appreciation* Day. You don't have to like it, just appreciate it. Like a great actor who's a jerk in real life."

Another amused little smile. He never gave big ones. "Okay then."

"Okay then. Here's my contribution; tell me if you can appreciate it. Ready?"

"Ready."

"I survived the crash because I wanted to die. My husband died because he wanted to live." I splayed my hands. "What do you think?"

•   •   •

"The doctor said I'd survived because I'd been asleep," I said. "My body had been limp, and this allowed me to walk away from it all with only a few bumps and bruises. My husband died because he was rigid when the car rolled. His body was like glass in a dryer, mine like a rag.

"Here's the thing, why the doctor is half-right: I wasn't asleep—I told the doctor I'd *been* asleep, but I wasn't. I was awake, and I knew exactly what was going to happen moments before that drunk in his truck T-boned us. I knew what was going to happen, and I didn't fight it. I let go." I gave that helpless little chuckle people do when the only other alternative was to cry. "I let go, and I lived because of it. The truck had even struck my side, the passenger side. And yet still Mike was killed—almost instantly, I was told."

Dr. Cole scribbled something in his notebook and then placed his attention back on me.

"I've heard of things like that before," I continued. "You know, like when a sky diver's chute doesn't open, they faint from fear, then hit the ground limp and live because of it."

"Except you didn't faint," Dr. Cole said.

"No."

"You were awake for it all."

"Yes."

"Why did you tell the doctor you'd been asleep?"

"I don't know. It seemed convenient."

"A more palatable tale to steer concern away from the truth?"

"Exactly. If I'd died in the accident, it wouldn't have been suicide—it would have been vehicular manslaughter. Not my fault. Not suicide."

"The opportunity you'd been hoping for."

"I—yes."

"You believe that your ability to see the accident moments before it happened, thus *allowing* it to happen, would somehow absolve you from the religious concerns you have about suicide?"

I knew what he was getting at. "You're saying it's still suicide."

Dr. Cole rarely said yes or no; he posed questions with attainable answers and waited for you. So I went.

"If you'd seen the things I have over the course of my career, never mind the goings-on in my own so-called life, you would certainly understand why I find the notion of heaven and hell—*all of it*—ludicrous. But I was baptized Catholic. I was taught that suicides go to hell. If there's even the slightest chance that's true, that something like heaven and hell do exist..."

"Then you would never see your son again, assuming you took your own life." He then added, with what I thought was equal parts logic and concern: "Or allowed someone to take it for you."

"Yes," I conceded softly. "If Christopher's up there waiting for me..."

"With his father now," he added.

"Right."

A brief pause.

"I imagine you were on a full dose of the drug the day of the crash?" he asked.

"Yes."

"Which would explain why you were able to see the accident moments before it happened," he said, not asked.

Still, I replied: "Yes."

"And what prompted you to take a full dose that day? It's been three weeks since we began tapering. You've been doing well."

"Mike and I had a fight," I said.

"About?"

"The usual. Christopher's passing. Me being dead inside, unable to move on."

"You took a full dose to help you cope after the fight?"

"Yes and no. We'd done nothing *but* fight since Christopher started getting bad; I'm used to that. But we were going out that night. It was"—I snorted at the notion—"an attempt at a new beginning."

"So you took the drug to help you cope with the evening out?"

I shrugged. "I guess it was both—the fight *and* the evening out."

"How soon after ingesting the drug did your senses become as acute as they do?"

"I don't know; it's different every time." I gave it more thought. I remembered smelling dog crap at a stoplight on the way to the restaurant. The windows were up. I looked around and saw no dogs, but figured it didn't necessarily mean there wasn't one—or its breakfast—nearby. At the next light, maybe two blocks up, there was a guy cleaning up after his dog. The smell was so strong at that point I almost gagged. "An hour maybe?" I eventually added, sparing Dr. Cole the dog shit story.

"What sense triggered the loudest alarm before the truck hit you?" he asked.

"I don't know. Sometimes it feels like all of them sound at once."

Dr. Cole dropped his eyes, not his head, and scribbled more in his notebook.

. . .

"You mentioned Agent Morris before we officially started," he said.

"Yes."

"He came to see you in the hospital?"

"Yes."

"To see whether you were all right."

I nodded.

"And that was all?"

I hated when he did this. He was like a parent waiting for their kid to tell the truth.

"No. He asked for my help."

"You're on sick leave."

"He wasn't officially asking me to come back."

"No?"

I shook my head. "I'd be like a consultant. At least until I was"—I made air quotes with both hands—"'ready to return.'"

"His words?"

"They weren't mine."

"Why do you think he needs you as a"—his turn at air quotes—"'consultant'? The Bureau has more than its share of competent agents for dealing with serial murder."

I raised an eyebrow at him. He knew why. And he knew *I* knew why. Yet there he sat, waiting for me to say it. Maybe it was a necessary part of my therapy I hadn't yet grasped.

I gave him what he wanted. "You and Morris are the only ones who know about the drug's effect on me," I said.

"Agent Morris knows the *positive* effect. He's unaware of the side effects."

"What happens to me when I take it *is* a side effect," I said.

"You know what I mean, Maggie."

Yes, I did. Regular use of the drug caused a whole bunch of unpleasant side effects. Hyperlipidemia, high blood pressure, diarrhea (having no social life helps with that one), type 2 diabetes, insomnia. Many people in the trial had dropped out. I stayed because the drug was the only thing—and I'd tried them all—that actually got me out of bed in the morning. Forever indebted to me (his words), Dr. Cole had reluctantly agreed to treat my side effects with more drugs. And of course they too had their side effects, didn't they? Talk about robbing Peter to pay Paul.

I'd promised Dr. Cole I'd start tapering down from a full dose of the drug to see whether we could find a therapeutic level that managed fewer side effects. And I had been. And it was going… okay, I guess. But after the fight with Mike, I guess you could say I fell off the wagon. And now here I was, asking my doctor of all people for another fix.

· · ·

"Apparently, they're stuck on one," I said. "A bad one."

Dr. Cole sat back in his chair and sighed, silently acknowledging my diversion. He allowed it, though. "How bad?"

"Five so far. All men."

"Is that uncommon?"

"Depends on how you interpret the odds." And then before I realized the implications of what I was about to say: "Presently, women account for about seventy percent of known victims of serial killers."

Dr. Cole did not look away, but his eyes flinched for a second. I admired his control. Always have. At the trial, he was given a chance to speak about his wife and Thomas Hays, and he was exceptionally composed. In case you haven't been paying attention, I've been a mess since losing Christopher. If cancer was a man, I'd have shot him stone dead at his trial, no question.

I did not address or apologize for the accidental reference I'd made. I was, after all, responding to his question with a fact. Dr. Cole knew this. A blink later and it was like it never happened. "And what is this serial predator's M.O.?" he asked.

"Well, that's the thing—it's still murky. Each victim died from blunt-force trauma. And it's excessive too; he really does a number on them."

"Which indicates rage, a lack of control."

"Right. Except to abduct all of these men—to do what he's done—requires premeditation. It's not impulsive."

"If all you have are five men who have been beaten to death, how can the Bureau be so sure they're dealing with the same culprit?"

"All victims were found cuffed behind the back, and the ligature marks on the wrists are extreme. This likely means that the victims weren't just cuffed and dispatched quickly. He did something with them while they were cuffed—something that made them want to shred their wrists down to the bone in an effort to get away."

Dr. Cole made a subtle but disturbed face as though he envisioned raw bone.

"They also found cuts on the right palm of each victim. Not the left, only the right. Lab reports say the cuts are more like punctures. Surrounding bruises on the palm suggest the victims had something jagged pressed into the hand until it poked through the flesh. Very weird."

"Could it be drug-related?" Dr. Cole asked.

"Doubtful. Drug traffickers usually prefer to display their victims to send a message. All five of these men were carefully dumped in hopes they wouldn't be found. Not to mention the profiles of the victims wouldn't fit such a theory."

"And what are the profiles? What are the similarities?"

"Apparently there are none, or at least none that we can see. Youngest was a nineteen-year-old college junior in southeastern Pennsylvania; oldest was a sixty-five-year-old accountant in upstate New York. College kid was blond and blue, accountant bald and brown."

"And Agent Morris still believes he's dealing with serial murder."

"Yeah. His gut's got a pretty decent track record."

"So does yours." Dr. Cole's eyes didn't flinch this time. When he's the one mentioning his wife, his composure is always stone; only when her murder is alluded to, catching him off guard, does he show the faintest crack.

But now he's prepared to talk about her, I thought. *Give him just enough.*

"Thomas Hays was a power whore," I said. "A desperate need to be at the center of it all is what did him in. It's what does a lot of them in."

"There was much more to it than that, Maggie."

He was angling for more than just enough. I wondered whether we should switch seats.

"Yeah, I guess there was," I said.

Dr. Cole placed his pen in his notebook and folded it shut. He did not need notes to remember what I was about to say.

. . .

"Hays was a sadist," I said. "He carved symbols into his victims before strangling them. Nonsense symbols he'd created that he would then translate to law enforcement via taunting letters. Like I said, classic power whore." I was looking for the flinch in his eyes as I spoke. I didn't see it. He already knew the details of the case, but this was the first we'd spoken of it. Much as I'm not fond of referring to myself as such, he was getting it straight from the horse's mouth.

"Since we'd found no indication of trophies being taken from the victims, I came up with the slim possibility that he was getting these same symbols tattooed onto his body in order to remember his victims intimately."

"This slim possibility just occurred to you out of the blue?" he asked. "There was no trigger?"

It sounded like he emphasized "slim." Like I wasn't giving myself enough credit.

"No—not out of the blue," I said. "I was in a restaurant with a friend. We had a drink at the bar while we waited for our table. My friend had a thing for the bartender. His sleeves were partially rolled up his forearms, and she spotted a tattoo peeking out. It was some kind of abstract design; you couldn't really tell what it was. So she asked him about it, and he rolled his sleeve farther up, revealing a pair of angel wings. He said his sister died last year, and the angel wings were so she would be with him always.

"Well, my friend nearly hopped the bar and jumped the guy's bones then and there, hot *and* sensitive being the Holy Grail that it is. And you know what? If she actually had, I'd never have noticed—I was in another world entirely, obsessing over what that bartender had said about keeping his sister with him always; the fact that we couldn't tell what his tattoo was at first, what it meant.

"I think I mumbled an apology to my friend after that, slapped money on the bar, and took off." I shrugged. "She ended up going home with the bartender, so I was forgiven."

Dr. Cole gave my wit a courtesy smile but remained quiet, waiting for me to continue.

"We began checking tattoo shops within the vicinity of where the bodies had been dumped," I said. "Showed them pictures of the symbols and asked whether any recent clients had gotten work done that resembled any of the symbols in our photos."

"And you got a hit on one of the shops," he said.

"We got a hit on several. Hays wasn't *that* stupid; he did have the presence of mind to go to different artists. Still, we got him."

"Did he use his real name and address on the releases he was required to fill out for the tattoo parlors?"

"No. But he did use Thomas as a first name at one shop, and Hays as a surname at another. He couldn't help himself."

"And you were able to piece that together?"

"Nope. Hays freaked the last tattoo artist out. Started going on about women and how there was only one real way to control them.

When the artist asked him what that 'way' was he said Hays just grinned at him. The kind of grin that made a two-hundred-and-fifty-pound guy covered in tattoos get the willies. So the artist—bless the guy—made sure to get the make and model of Hays's car as he was leaving. After that, it didn't take long."

"You made the arrest."

"Yes."

An awkward quiet followed. Dr. Cole offered me tea, and I accepted. He left for a few minutes to prepare it.

.   .   .

When Dr. Cole returned with the tea, I asked: "Why were you asking me about all that, Dr. Cole? It can't be pleasant for you."

"It's not. But I need you to see that your investigative work, unlike your depression over the loss of your son, isn't dependent on a drug."

"I know that. It sure as hell speeds things up, though."

He pursed his lips. "Maggie…"

I carried on, undeterred. "You remember when I helped Morris not long after Christopher died?"

"Yes."

"I was in no shape to do any investigative thinking. No shape. I couldn't even follow the stupidest of TV shows. Morris had stopped by, insisting I get out of the house for a bit. The drug was helping me cope a tiny bit better by then, so I agreed. I don't remember how we ended up at his crime scene; maybe he was thinking of something to occupy my mind while avoiding the subject of Christopher. I appreciated that. One more sympathetic-eyed visitor crooning, 'How you holding up, Maggie?' and I would have opened fire."

"You found a crucial bit of evidence at his scene that everyone else had missed," he said.

"I did. They probably would have found it eventually, I just found it quicker."

"You *heard* it," Dr. Cole said.

"Yeah. The flow of air through one of the heating grates in the bedroom sounded…off, like something was obstructing it."

"They found the murder weapon hidden in the heating duct."

"Yup. Morris was dumbfounded. Everyone was. I told them I'd heard a rattle, even though I hadn't; I'd only heard a faint disruption in the flow of air when the heat clicked on. I later told Morris the truth. I'm not sure he believed me at first, and I didn't blame him. But he couldn't argue with what he'd seen, and he surely didn't suspect *me* of hiding the murder weapon in there. Later that night, I told him about the drug and how I suspected it was responsible for all of these weird effects on my senses I'd been experiencing. I'm not sure he totally bought into it, but he was grateful for my assistance that day."

"He's buying into it now," Dr. Cole said.

"I think he's getting desperate."

"And you still insist on giving the drug full credit for your discovery at Morris's crime scene?"

"How could I not? It would be impossible for a person to actually *hear*—" I stopped and sighed, deciding to change my approach. "The drug is the reason you're not sitting across from an empty chair today, Dr. Cole. Please tell me the delicious bit of irony about who survived the crash—and *why*—hasn't escaped you already."

"No, it hasn't," he said evenly. "So am I to assume you're willing to deal with the other side effects that come with daily use of a full dose? The negative effects?"

"With your help. You can treat them like you did before."

Dr. Cole looked away for a moment. "And what if the drug ultimately kills you? Does your knowledge of the drug's harmful side effects not make you culpable in the event of your death?"

He was talking suicide again. And I guess he was right; I'd never considered this point of view. But Morris had said something when he visited me at the hospital. Something that had practically made up my mind on the spot. I repeated his words to Dr. Cole as though they were my own: "All things considered, I only recently realized that I was fortunate—the last face Christopher saw before he died was mine. He felt loved, he felt safe, and I made sure he felt no pain." Now it was my turn to look away; the guilt for what I was about to say to Dr. Cole made eye contact impossible. "The monsters I hunt...they ensure their victims experience the total and complete opposite of that."

Dr. Cole left his office and returned with a six-month supply of the drug. His eyes were red. My guilt on the drive home made me sicker than the drug ever would.

CHAPTER 3

I went straight to the bar after leaving Dr. Cole. Morris was waiting for me at a small table in back. He was drinking scotch. He was usually a light-beer guy, and not many at that.

"How'd it go?" he asked as I took a seat across from him.

"I feel dirty," I said.

"Why?"

I looked around to see whether a waiter was floating nearby or whether I needed to go to the bar to get a drink. "There a waiter?"

"No." Morris drained his scotch and then started crunching on a piece of ice. "I got a tab going at the bar, though." He slid his empty glass towards me. "Here, get me another."

I frowned. "Gee, can I, mister?"

"I buy, you fly. You know the rules."

I muttered "asshole" and went up to the bar.

·   ·   ·

The bartender, a cute guy with nice arms and what I would soon confirm to be a nice butt when he turned to fix our drinks, smiled as I approached. Though sex seemed like something I'd done in another life, my libido wasn't completely dead. On life support, yes, but not completely dead. Although now that I was about to go back on a full dose of the drug, they might as well pull the plug. Complete loss of libido—and I mean complete loss, one step shy of picking up your copy of *So, You're Asexual*—is yet another lovely side effect of the drug.

"Same again for him—" I gestured back at Morris. "And I'll have a chardonnay, please." The bartender turned, showed me that nice butt, and went to work on our drinks. When he returned, I pointed to the scotch he'd just poured. "How many is that for him?"

"That's his third, I think."

It was only 12:30.

"Good ole three-martini lunch, right?" I said with a smile.

The bartender looked at me, the drink, and then back at me. "That's scotch," he said.

I sighed inside. Well, you didn't take home a guy like that to talk, did you? "Right," I said. "Thanks." I took the drinks and headed back to the table.

.   .   .

"So why dirty?" Morris asked.

I sipped my chardonnay. "Because I feel like I manipulated him to get what I wanted."

"You manipulated *him*? You go on about him like he's Einstein."

"He is. But there's always a button somewhere; you know that."

Morris sipped his scotch and then looked at me with a face that already knew the answer. "You mentioned his wife."

I took a healthy pull from my chardonnay. "Yeah."

"You tell him what I told you?"

"You mean when you found *my* button?" I locked eyes with him, refusing to blink first.

He looked away. "Wasn't hard to find."

"Neither was Dr. Cole's. It doesn't make it any less of a dick move, Tim. And it doesn't make me feel any less dirty."

Morris drained his scotch and started crunching ice again. "You wanna back out, go ahead."

"No, I don't."

"So then what the hell, Maggie?"

Maggie? It was always Mags. He wasn't being himself. Either he had a good buzz going, or he was stressing more than usual over this one. Or both. Likely both.

I played male and decided to ignore the issue until it went away.

"All right—so tell me about this one," I said.

"Already told you most."

"Five so far. All men. No discernible—"

"Six," he said.

I leaned back in my chair and sighed. This explained the three-martini lunch.

. . .

"When did you get the call?"

"About an hour ago."

"How old?"

"No positive ID yet. They're guessing mid-thirties. Brown and brown. Short and thin. Still no pattern."

"Where'd they find him?"

"Upstate Pennsylvania."

"Who reported it?"

"Anonymous call."

I leaned forward in my chair—

"No," Morris said quickly, snuffing my optimism. "No, the bastard's still keeping his ego in check. Turns out a bunch of teens drinking in the woods spotted him."

"They were worried about the underage drinking, so they phoned it in anonymously," I said.

He did a *bingo* touch on the tip of his nose. "Finding a dead body, though, at that age? In a town where a good night is scoring cheap beer and going cow tipping? They weren't keeping that secret long."

I nodded in agreement. I grew up in a rural town in Iowa. Your only escape to the outside world was television. To be the kid in school who found a dead body like the ones on TV or in the movies? Hell, we're talking a mega climb up the Podunk pop charts.

"So," I continued, "cuffed from behind?"

"Yeah. Gagged too."

"Gagged?"

Morris nodded. Gagged was a new wrinkle.

"Blunt-force trauma the cause of death?" I asked.

"Yeah—but he didn't go caveman on him like he did the others."

"He didn't?"

Morris shook his head. "Looks like he hit him just enough to do the job."

"Wounds on the right palm?" I asked.

"No."

"*No?* So it might not be him."

Morris looked annoyed. "It's him."

I didn't argue. "Okay, it's him. Tell me more."

"We're thinking the murder weapon was a shovel."

"Why?"

"Forensics. Not to mention kids found the body in a makeshift grave."

"Come again?"

"Bastard dug a grave out in the middle of the woods. We think the kids interrupted him and he took off before he could finish burying the guy."

I processed this. "Some things don't add up."

"Go."

"Well, how about why bury him? He didn't go to such lengths with his other victims."

"My guess is he didn't want this one found."

"Maybe. But to haul a dead body into the woods, plop him down, and start digging a hole? Hardly a time management guru, this guy."

"He could've had the hole dug beforehand. Plus you're assuming the guy was already dead when he took him out there."

"Why wouldn't I? Is he gonna drag a writhing body through the woods? Risky."

"You're forgetting the gag. If he was already dead, there'd be no need for a gag."

True.

Morris started eyeing up the bar. "That and time of death. Wasn't too far off from when the kids found him."

I rolled my eyes, annoyed. "You could have just said, jackass."

I saw the flash of a smirk. This was the old Morris—driving me nuts and loving it. I felt sad the smirk was so fleeting.

I said: "All right, so let's say he drags the guy—*alive*—out to his grave in the woods. The guy's bound and gagged. The hole is already dug; the shovel is already there."

"Okay…"

"He's getting ready to do…something, but the kids come along and ruin whatever it is. So he's forced to bash the guy in the head quickly and take off, no typical caveman job, no chance to do whatever the hell he does to their right palms."

Morris took his eyes off the bar, started playing. "He's angry, frustrated now. He didn't get to fulfill his fantasy."

"And what *is* his fantasy? What was he planning to do to this guy that is similar to all the others? Was he planning to bury him alive?"

"He never bothered to bury the others. And alive? Pretty damn macabre."

"Yeah, that would be mean."

He grunted at my sarcasm.

I added: "Hell, my own brother used to cocoon me in a quilt and then stuff me in the closet because he knew I was claustrophobic."

"Charming brother."

"He was the nicest of the three."

"So is that why you're such a big bad federal agent girl? Trying to fit in while growing up in such a patriarchal family? Please Daddy and all that?"

"I can't believe they let you lecture psych at the academy."

"What was Mom like?" he asked me.

I hesitated before settling on: "Compliant."

Morris could tell his ribbing had inadvertently struck a nerve. He went quiet for a moment and started eyeing up the bar again.

•   •   •

"No trophies," I said, eager to move on.

"None that we can tell."

"So we've got six now. All men. All Caucasian?"

Morris let out a dejected chuckle. "Of course not. Fourth was a black guy from Maryland."

I continued as though this news wasn't the deterrent it was. "All men, no ethnic prejudice, and no age prejudice; you mentioned one was a college kid and one was an accountant in his sixties, right?"

He nodded.

"That alone could be significant," I said.

"Tell me."

"Well, he's not going for easy ones, is he? College kid? Accountant? Hardly pros and drifters. What about the black guy from Maryland?"

"Software sales. Married with two kids."

"And the other three?"

"They were not pros and drifters."

I started to theorize a different picture, a picture I knew Morris would refuse: Perhaps this was not serial murder we were dealing with after all. Maybe the motives were more financial or vengeful than hedonistic, the victims more assigned than chosen or opportunistic. Who's to say college boy's tuition wasn't going up his nose? His tuition eventually runs out, but by then he's already run up too big a tab on the wrong people.

Who's to say the sixty-something accountant didn't spend his off-season clutching a bookie's ankle, begging for one more week to make good until they'd finally had enough?

And the software family man from Maryland. Perhaps his wife found out he wasn't quite the family man he was pretending to be. Perhaps her rage at his infidelity saw her placing retribution into the hands of a professional.

And what, Maggie, the dealer, the bookie, and the scorned wife just happened to hire the same hitman? A guy who cuffed his targets behind the back before bashing their heads into goo? Left a crude hallmark on their right palms?

No. Ridiculous odds. Besides, a professional would never be so messy. True professionals are ghosts, at home and in bed before their victims hit the floor.

I then considered a visionary motive. A psychotic who believes he is doing something like God's work perhaps. The victims were all demons in his eyes or some other crazy shit only he could understand.

Maybe.

Or maybe Morris's gut—full of scotch as it was—had intended on extending its winning streak. He was tired, his SAC (Special Agent in Charge) was catching a lot of shit on this one (which of course meant Morris was catching a lot of shit on this one), but a better agent in this field I didn't know. If Morris had even the tiniest inkling that this was something other than serial murder, we wouldn't be here discussing it.

I sipped my chardonnay. "I'm just a consultant here, Tim. *Your* consultant. Hush-hush and all that for now if you want. It's obvious you're working up to something, so out with it."

His gaze stayed fixed on the bar.

I sighed, pushed back my chair, and stood. "I'll get you another."

"No," he said, eyes clicking back on me. It was then I realized that his constant gaze on the bar was entirely coincidental; his mind had been churning, plotting our first move. "Let's head upstate and have a look at that grave."

CHAPTER 4

Trenton, New Jersey

Hal Redmond sat in the alley, thumbing through an old issue of *People* magazine. He flipped to a page featuring Jennifer Aniston and marveled at her beauty. "In the next life," he said, gently touching her face with a soiled finger. "In the next life."

Hal turned the page but stopped reading. Someone was watching him; he was sure of it. Years of living on the street had given him the foresight of a feral cat. He set the magazine aside and instinctively clutched the canvas backpack that held his life.

Hal scanned the alley. He saw no one at first—and that was the point for his being there, really. It was nearly four o'clock and the alley emptied around this time; competition at the soup kitchen could be fierce the moment the doors opened for supper. Hal had chosen to stay behind today, wanted to read his *People* magazine in peace. Most of the guys he shared the alley with were young punks, disrespectful pigs—he knew what they'd do with the magazine and Jennifer Aniston's pretty picture if they got hold of it. And for a moment, Hal thought that was what this was all about; the feeling of being watched was someone keen to grab his magazine. After all, nobody looked at the homeless for more than a blink—except other homeless.

Hal quickly shoved the magazine into his bag and stood. He fixed his stare on the west end of the empty alley that led out into the street. "Who's there?"

A silver Toyota Camry rolled into view. The window came down and revealed the face of a smiling, clean-cut white man.

Lost, Hal instantly thought. The only white boys around here were white boys like Hal—and this guy was not a white boy like Hal.

Someone from the soup kitchen maybe? Letting him know that if he waited much longer, they wouldn't be able to guarantee him a meal? No. They liked Hal at the kitchen, but they wouldn't go to such lengths.

Cop? No. This guy was too wholesome looking, his smile too trusting.

That left lost or crazy. Hal wanted no part of either.

"Evening," the man said, still smiling.

Hal only nodded.

"I'm a little lost…" The man looked out his passenger window, then back at Hal with a chuckle. "Actually, *a lot* lost."

"Yeah, I can see that," Hal said. "Sun won't be up much longer. You should leave now, mister."

The man chuckled again. "Well, how can I leave if I don't know where I am?"

"Not my problem." Hal turned to leave.

"*Wait*. Money and a hot meal if you help me get out of here. Even a warm bed if you want."

Hal turned back to the man. "I'm not into no rough trade, mister."

The man held up a hand. "Whoa, you misunderstand, my friend. I'm not looking for anything like that. All I need is someone to get me outta here—I feel like I've been going in circles. I was just offering compensation if you helped me. I'll pay you whatever you think's fair." The man's smile finally left for a more appropriate look of anxiety.

"I'll give you directions, mister, but I ain't getting in your car."

"I've already gotten directions—*three times*. You can see how much good they did me. What I need is someone to *show* me."

"Sorry, mister." Hal turned to leave again.

"*Please.*"

Hal stopped, sighed, then turned back around. He pegged the man as a typical suburbanite who'd wandered too far from his picket fence. If he left a guy like that to continue driving around aimlessly in this part of town, it would only be a matter of time until he was a statistic.

The man was offering a hot meal. Since Hal had chosen solitude over a good spot in line at the soup kitchen tonight, it was a damn tempting offer. Hal could get him to hit up a drive-thru and buy him half a dozen—heck, a *dozen*—burgers. Enough to last him the week. The man also said he'd pay whatever Hal wanted. That was nice. Cash was always nice.

Still, so many crazies around these days, so many perverts, suburbanite or not. In fact, it seemed like all the real crazies Hal read about were creepy white guys *from* the 'burbs.

"How much money we talking?" Hal asked.

The man quickly dug into his pocket and produced a thick wad of bills. "You can have it all. Just get me the heck out of here, please."

Hal gaped at the wad as though it were Jennifer Aniston herself. Even if the wad contained all ones, it was more than Hal would see in months.

A dozen burgers and a pocket full of cash. If he didn't take it, someone else would. And then a voice in his head, both genuine and with a selfish need for justification: *And that someone else just might kill the poor fool.*

"I get all of that?" Hal asked.

"All of it."

"Dinner too?"

"Absolutely."

"You try and mess with me, it'll be the last thing your lily-white ass ever does, mister."

The man shook his head adamantly. "No, no, never—never."

Hal nodded. "All right then, mister."

The man started smiling again.

CHAPTER 5

Hal woke disoriented. His head ached like he'd had too much whiskey. Except he hadn't; he knew he hadn't. He'd only had the few belts he'd been offered when he got into the man's car.

The man.

The white man in the alley.

The man who said he was lost and needed help getting out of Trenton. It was coming back to him now...

Hal remembered getting into the car with the man. He remembered the man immediately handing over the wad of cash, thanking Hal repeatedly. He remembered the man offering Hal a swig from a half-empty pint of Jack, the man taking a swig first, silently assuring Hal it was safe.

His next memory was waking up here.

Hal stood. Something clanked at his feet. What the hell? He bent to inspect. A shackle was on his right ankle. The shackle was chained to one of four concrete walls. A strip of fluorescent light buzzed overhead, ugly in its effort at showcasing the room. Not that any other lighting might have done a better job; there was little to work with. The room was akin to a large jail cell. A solitary door—not made of bars like a cell, but rather a solid piece of what appeared to be steel—was directly ahead. To the left of the door was a small window. The shades were drawn.

Hal shuffled forward, the chain on his ankle clinking behind and then abruptly stopping his shuffle as it reached the end of its length. The door was still a good ten feet away. Hal bent and gripped the chain, giving it a strong tug to test its strength. He felt no give at all. He dropped the chain with a definitive clank and rubbed his aching head.

What in the hell? Hal thought. *A thousand times, what in the holy hell?* "Hello!? Anyone there!? *Hello!?*"

A metallic clank from the steel door, followed by the sound of a heavy bolt sliding free. The door opened. The white man he'd offered to help entered, shutting the steel door behind him. The man was carrying a large burlap sack and smiling the same inappropriate smile he'd flashed when they'd met in the alley.

"Hi, Hal," the man said. "How are you feeling?"

"My head hurts."

"Yeah, I thought it might. Sorry about that."

"What'd you do to me, man? Where am I? What the hell is this?"

The man chuckled and patted the air with a hand. "Slow down, Hal...just slow down."

Hal bent and tugged at the chain on his ankle again, more an unspoken demand for an explanation than a means of escape.

"You're not going anywhere, Hal. And to save your lungs the time and effort—" The man suddenly screamed, a powerful five-second burst that reverberated throughout the room, punishing Hal's head further still. The man then stopped and calmly continued with: "No one's going to hear if you try to scream for help."

Hal raised his chin, defiant. "I ain't never screamed for nothing in my life."

The man could scarcely contain his joy. He closed his eyes and tilted his head skyward with a breathless grin. Hal thought he looked like a man receiving oral sex from an invisible woman. For a brief moment, the image disturbed him more than his predicament.

The man lowered his head. "You have no idea how happy I am to hear that, Hal." The man's joy then slowly dissipated as he went on. "I had such a great one planned last night. I'd been working on it for some time." He set the burlap sack on the floor and leaned against the steel door. "You know how many times I scouted that area? *Dozens*. Not a single soul each time." He snorted. "Million to one those kids coming along when they did. Million to one."

Hal remained silent. The man's ramblings were a crazy man's. And not the kind of crazy Hal had seen on the street over the years. This man was a whole different kind of nuts.

"No offense, but you were kind of a consolation prize, Hal," the man went on. "I was going to try to make the best of it, but my hopes weren't too high. However, what you said to me on the ride here—"

What I said on the ride here???

"—and what you said to me just now makes me think I might have something after all."

"What did I say on the ride here?"

"You don't remember?"

"No."

The man started to laugh. "I'm sorry, Hal, that was mean; I didn't expect you to remember. That whiskey wasn't exactly pure."

"You drank some," Hal said.

"I *pretended* to drink some. Geez, come on, Hal. Not one for common sense, are you? No, I guess not..." The man started laughing again. "You wouldn't be here if you were."

"What do you want?" Hal asked.

The man's laughing stopped. His smile dropped like a stone. "A real man has common sense."

"Whatever you say."

The man's face remained grave. "So you've never screamed from anything before, huh?"

"*No*. And I ain't about to start now neither, boy."

Lightswitch-quick the man's grave expression became a smile again. He bent and opened the burlap sack, removing items and placing them on the floor. One of the items was a pair of handcuffs.

Hal spit and said: "Good luck gettin' those on me, boy."

"Oh, I don't believe I'll need luck." The man removed the final item from the sack and placed it on the floor, the breathless, almost sexual grin once again emblazoned across his face, giddy for reward.

And Hal gave it to the man instantly. He couldn't help it. The final item terrified him to his core.

CHAPTER 6

Towanda, Pennsylvania

The crime scene was in a remote wooded area in the rural town of Towanda. Definitely out there. Morris held up the police tape for me. I thanked him and ducked under. We stood side by side without speaking for a tick, taking it all in. The initial responding officers had done a good job at blocking the area off and setting up grids. Morris immediately took me to grid block A—the grave where the teenage boozers had found the body.

One of two officers on the scene left his partner and approached us. He was holding a notebook and a thick folder in his left hand. "You the guys who called ahead?"

"Agent Morris." Morris shook his hand, then paused for a second as he thought how to address me. "This is Maggie Allen…she's a consultant on the case."

"Detective Sill." He finished with Morris and then took my hand. "You guys mind signing in?"

Morris and I both said no at the same time, then took turns signing our names in Detective Sill's notebook. Sill thanked us, then handed the thick folder he'd been holding over to Morris. "Here's the file."

Morris smiled politely. "Thank you."

Detective Sill flicked his chin back towards the other detective. "We were about to go grab a bite. You need anything before we go?"

Morris held up a hand. "I think we're good, thanks."

"We shouldn't be long."

"Take your time…" Morris scanned the full perimeter of the crime scene and gave an admiring little nod Detective Sill couldn't miss. "Looks like you guys could *use* a break."

"Got that right," Detective Sill said. "Nice to meet you both. Let us know if you find anything, alright?"

"Absolutely."

Detective Sill rejoined the second detective. The two of them spoke in a huddle for a minute, the second detective shooting me, not Morris, a quick glance as he listened to Detective Sill.

.   .   .

When they were gone, I asked Morris: "Your lips feeling chapped?"

"There's a difference between kissing ass and greasing the wheels."

"Since when do we have to grease local wheels?"

"You gonna make me come up with a whole rusty-cog-in-the-machine analogy? The days of federal and local being all tight-lipped to one another are pretty much over, but it still happens. You know that. I'd rather go in chummy. If they insist on being assholes and pocketing leads in order to get the collar, *then* we throw our weight around. That okay with you?"

"You see the way that other detective looked at me?"

"Probably has a thing for annoying redheads."

"Or maybe they're wondering just what the hell constitutes a consultant for this kind of thing."

"Better I tell them you're an agent currently on bereavement? I'm sure that wouldn't cause a stir at their next briefing."

"'*Looks like you guys could* use *a break*,'" I mocked.

Morris shook his head and looked down into the grave. I bit back a smirk and looked down too. It felt good to be out in the field. Maybe it was the drug kicking in, or maybe it was because I was keeping my head busy, not allowing it to sit in bed for days at a time ruminating about Christopher, feeling as though I might literally succumb to heartache.

Morris glanced over at me as I was looking down. Dusk was still a good twenty or so minutes away, so I imagined he was using the light to get a good read on my face, a blended gaze of both professional and personal curiosity; he'd seen me take the drug on the drive here, and I figured he was now studying me to see if and how I was going to pull a sudden Houdini out of my butt.

"Can I help you?" I said, my eyes still on the grave.

He didn't seem to care I'd noticed him staring. "Anything?" he asked.

"Doesn't work like that, Tim."

"So how does it work, exactly?"

"If I knew, we'd have the guy already. Just let me do my thing, all right?"

Morris turned and started surveying the crime scene on his own, periodically thumbing through the file.

My thing, I thought. *Whatever the hell that is.*

I remained at the grave and closed my eyes. I took a deep breath through my nose and let it out slowly through my mouth.

Just listen, smell, and feel. Open your eyes and look too. No, keep them closed for now. Keep still. Whenever it's happened before, you never had to do anything; everything presented itself.

Just stand here and be still. Let it happen.

Be still...

Still...

Sti—

Fire shot up my nose. I recoiled and spun, my eyes watering instantly.

Morris was immediately at my side, rubbing my back and consoling me. "You all right? You all right?"

I nodded and stood upright, wiping the tears from my eyes. My nostrils burned.

"What is it?" Morris insisted.

"Alcohol," I said. "Isopropyl alcohol. It feels like I just snorted it."

"Isoprop—rubbing alcohol?"

I nodded, still wiping my eyes, still massaging my nose.

Morris started flipping through the file, silently mouthing the words "isopropyl alcohol" over and over as he did so.

I pushed the file out of his face and placed my hand on his chest. "Take my hand," I said.

"What?"

I closed my eyes. "Take my hand. Go where I say, and make sure I don't trip on anything."

I could feel the uncertainty in his grip, and for a moment I thought he was going to pull away and ask more questions. Instead, he did as I asked him.

I told him to take me east. Then north. Then east again. When I told him to take us north some more, he stopped me.

"You're taking us outside the tape," he said.

I opened my eyes. We were almost touching the yellow tape. "So?"

Morris shrugged. "Just saying it's time to duck."

We ducked under the tape.

.   .   .

It didn't take long after that. Morris snapped on a pair of latex gloves and squatted down to retrieve a small square of black cloth. He stood and held it up to the fading light. The smell of rubbing alcohol was so strong I had to tuck my nose into my collar. My eyes started watering again.

Morris looked at me with more personal than professional curiosity this time, then brought his attention back to the square of cloth. "Microfiber cloth. Used on camera lenses and the like."

Nose still in my collar, I said: "That would explain the alcohol."

"Huh?"

I pulled my nose free. "*That would explain the smell of alcohol.* Clean the lens with the isopropyl and then dry it with the microfiber."

Morris lowered the cloth and looked at me. "So what are we saying here? Someone snapped a picture of our guy in action?"

"Doubtful," I said. "You think someone who happens upon a murder in the woods is going to stop and clean his or her lens first?"

"Maybe it was one of the teens who found him."

"No—they told us about the body. No reason to lie about catching it on film."

"There is if they were snapping pictures instead of trying to help the guy."

I took the file from Morris. I found the information I wanted and spoke with my eyes on the page. "Teens were heading north when they found the body. After coming clean, their statements were unanimous in that they headed back south to phone it in." I lifted my head and gestured to the cloth in Morris's hand. "We found that farther north, beyond the crime scene."

"*You* found it."

"You don't have to try anymore; I'm already on board."

Morris bit back a smile.

"So what do we have then?" I asked.

Morris held the dark square of cloth up to the fading light again. "Looks relatively new. Odds are slim it's been out here a while. Think you would have smelled the rubbing alcohol if it had?"

"No idea."

"Then we have a piece of microfiber cloth soaked in isopropyl alcohol about..." He turned back to the crime scene to gauge distance. "Five yards north of the crime scene." He glanced at me. "It could belong to our guy."

"Maybe."

"He could have used it for wiping down prints."

"Nah—our guy's too careful. To go without gloves and hope to clean up after would be foolish. Besides, microfiber cloths are pretty solid at removing prints without the aid of a cleanser. An isopropyl mixture would likely be used for something delicate, like a lens."

"Okay, a lens it is. Let's play."

"Go."

"Option A," Morris began. "The cloth *is* days old and belongs to a shutterbug who was taking a walk through the woods, snapping up nature or whatever. He dropped the cloth and never noticed."

"Very likely. Option B?"

"Some other shutterbug is in the woods, except he's clicking away *last night*. He stops to clean his lens with an isopropyl alcohol-based cleanser and a microfiber cloth, but then he sees something. Something that spooks him. Our guy and his victim."

I joined in now. "He jams his gear into his camera bag and hightails it out of there, keen on not being victim number two in the hole."

Morris: "But as he jams his gear into his bag, he drops the microfiber cloth. It's dark, the cloth is dark, and he doesn't notice. And even if he did, he doesn't give a shit—the cloth is cheap, his life is not."

"But did he get a picture before he bolted?" I asked. "And if so, is he planning on telling anyone?"

A brief pause.

"Something irks me about Option B," Morris eventually said.

"What?"

"Who the hell takes pictures of nature at night?"

"It's possible," I said. "Owls, foxes, raccoons... just need an infrared camera. Or maybe he wasn't even taking pictures of nature."

"Well, that makes even less sense then. What else would you take pictures of out here?" He waved a hand all over our forested surroundings.

"All right, Option B isn't as likely as Option A," I said. "How about Option C?"

"Option C," Morris said.

I waited.

"Option C..." Morris said again, looking uncertain whether he wanted to continue.

"Yeeeeessss...?"

"Option C—the microfiber cloth belongs to our guy."

"You had to second-guess that?" I asked.

"What's he need a camera for?"

"Scouting ahead? Making sure the area was secure enough to do his thing?"

"Yeah...maybe." He frowned. "So he sits back here and takes pictures, what—fifteen feet away—looking for the ideal spot to dig his grave? Why bother? It's fifteen feet."

"Maybe he was—" My surroundings disappeared. My whole world was suddenly a solitary page in the file, a page I had not consciously studied while flipping for the teens' statements, yet somehow it had registered all the same. It was the drug.

"What?" Morris said. "More? *You smell more?*"

I ignored him and immediately opened the file. Found the page I wanted and hurried back towards the crime scene.

"*What?*" Morris pleaded behind me as he followed.

I ducked under the tape and approached grid block D where a square of earth had been sectioned off a few feet from the base of the grave. It had been sectioned off because a manhole-sized circle had been cleared away among the surrounding foliage. It looked deliberate. Local PD thought it might have been a spot where the victim was kneeling before being struck with the shovel and then dumped into the hole.

.   .   .

I squatted and studied the circle. Morris loomed over me.

"You gonna tell me what the hell?" he said.

I handed the file up to him. "Read."

He did. "Local PD marked it off because it looked like a deliberate circle made in the earth. They're right too." He looked around. "The rest is completely carpeted with leaves and twigs."

"Local PD surmised this was where the victim was kneeling before being struck, thus the circle," I said.

"Yeah?"

"You kneel on the ground, it's going to flatten debris, not clear it," I said. "And a circle this big?" I spun an index finger over the spot.

"If he's kneeling long enough, squirming and shifting, doing his goddamnedest to escape the cuffs like all the others had, he could move things around," Morris said.

"Except this guy didn't have the extreme ligature marks on the wrists the others had, remember?" I got as close as I could without disturbing the evidence. "I don't see any indentation in the earth either. You're on your knees long enough to move stuff around and clear a big spot, you're going to leave a depression, yes?"

"Most likely."

I stood and backed up until the circle of earth was directly in front of me. Directly in front of that was the grave. I pulled my phone from my pocket, aimed it down at the grave, and snapped a picture. I then looked at my phone. I'd captured everything.

I handed the phone to Morris and said: "I think I know what his trophies are."

CHAPTER 7

Morris had given Detective Sill the microfiber cloth when he and his partner returned from dinner. I kept my theory about the killer's trophies between Morris and me for the time being, telling Sill and his team instead that it was likely—and it was, of course—that the cloth was best explained with Option A: It had been dropped by a guy or girl snapping pics of nature days ago, but they should keep on looking just in case.

Plausible as it was, Morris's veteran gut wasn't wild about Option A. He liked Option C—my theory. I was pleased. My gut liked my theory too.

·   ·   ·

And so now, sitting in the car while Detective Sill, his partner, and at least half a dozen flashlights were busy sweeping the newly expanded crime scene, Morris and I recapped my theory about the killer's trophies while sharing a box of Cheez-Its.

"So you think he cleared away the foliage on the ground to make room for a tripod," Morris said.

"Possibly. You saw the ground—lots of twigs, rocks. He'd want the tripod to be as steady as possible to capture his trophies, wouldn't he?"

"And he'd want the lens to be as clean as possible," Morris said, alluding to the microfiber cloth and the smell of rubbing alcohol.

"Right."

"But I didn't see any little holes in that circle he cleared, did you?" Morris said. "Little holes that the legs of a tripod might make? We didn't see *any* indentations in the circle, hence your ruling out local PD's theory about the victim kneeling before he was killed."

"Okay, so he clears the spot on the ground first, cleans his lens, but then gets interrupted before he can set the tripod up," I said.

Morris took the Cheez-It box out of my lap. "Okay then, he's interrupted, has to kill the guy quickly—"

"Why?" I interrupted.

"Huh?"

"Why kill him?" I said.

Morris frowned. "Because that's what he does."

"No—no, he *didn't* do what he does. No caveman job on the head, no marks on the right palm. Why take the chance of killing him *at all* when a group of teens are approaching? Why not just get the hell out of there ASAP?"

Morris's frown dissolved. He knew what I was getting at. "Because the victim could've ID'd him," he said.

"Exactly. Which could mean two things: One, our guy doesn't wear a mask or conceal his identity in any significant way. Or two, the victim *knew* our guy, which would make a decent answer to the 'why bury this one?' question. He didn't want any connection between him and the victim to be investigated."

Morris, munching away as I spoke, washed it down with a swig from his bottle of water and said: "I'm sold on the no mask thing. But I'm not so sold on the *he knew the guy* thing. Why would victim number six be someone he knew? It's too risky. Usually victim one has some kind of significance, not victims four, five, or six. And so far we've gotten zip on victim one."

"His cooling-off period between victims is getting shorter and shorter. Maybe this was opportunistic, something he couldn't pass up," I said.

"The grave had already been dug. That's premeditation at its best."

He was right. I took the Cheez-Its back and stuffed a handful into my mouth.

· · ·

"Let's stay with the evidence and your theory for a minute," he said. "Our guy has the victim cuffed and gagged and ready to go into the hole he'd already dug. This one, unlike the other five, was likely gagged because they were outdoors. That and time of death tells us the victim was still alive. It also tells us that the last five were killed someplace that offered exceptional privacy, a place where screaming would go unheard."

I chased my mouthful down from my own bottle of water and nodded.

Morris continued.

"All right, so he clears away a spot for his tripod, and then starts cleaning his camera lens with the alcohol and cloth before setting everything up. He hears the teens in the distance, panics, picks up the shovel, and whacks the victim just enough to do the job—nothing excessive—and then kicks him into the hole."

I came in. "He doesn't even have time to lob a few shovels of soil onto the victim. He packs up his gear lickety-split and bolts north, dropping the microfiber cloth en route."

"No time to snap photos or record video."

"And no time for the right palm to be damaged."

"His fantasy has been cut short. He's got metaphorical blue balls now."

I gave Morris a look that told him he was gross.

He rolled his eyes and amended it with: "He's *frustrated* now—does that mean we can expect another sooner than later to compensate?"

"I don't know."

Morris took the box of Cheez-Its from me. "I still wanna know what the grave was all about."

"Maybe he *didn't* know him, but it's certainly possible he was burying him because he didn't want him found."

"Why?"

"I don't know."

He cursed and flung a handful of Cheez-Its out the driver's side window.

"*Tim...*"

He exhaled, long and slow.

"Tree by tree, Tim," I said. "We start looking at the forest and we go nuts; you know that."

He nodded, keeping his gaze out the window. He handed the box of Cheez-Its back to me without looking.

"We caught a break today," I said, gesturing to all the bobbing flashlights in the distance. "Who knows what else they'll find now?"

He let out another long sigh. "I just wanna know what this guy is all about. All I know is that we have six now." He looked out his window again. His voice sounded detached, as though he wasn't aware he was thinking aloud. "The time to catch a guy like this is the first one or two, when he's still experimenting and unsure of himself, likely to be careless. *Six* now."

"He'll grow bolder," I said. "His confidence will get the better of him; he'll get reckless."

"Maybe. But to go through the trouble to dump his victims up and down the entire East Coast? To attempt to *bury* one? That's not a Thomas Hays whoring it up for the world; it's a guy who doesn't want to get caught." He sighed again. "A guy like that scares the hell out of me."

CHAPTER 8

It'd been three days since Morris and I had gone to the crime scene and found the microfiber cloth. Local PD had been worker bees in expanding the crime scene, looking for things they might have missed the first time around, but according to Morris's latest phone call, they'd found nothing more.

"Maybe we should head on back there," he suggested. "See if you can't find something else."

I was propped up in bed, channel surfing and eating stale Wheat Thins. To say my motivation was on the low side would have been a gross understatement. "I think I got everything there was to get," I said.

"How do you know? You said yourself you don't know how the drug works. Maybe it gave you all it could for *that day*. Maybe if we head back now, recharged so to speak, you can find something new."

I plucked a few Wheat Thins crumbs off my chest and nibbled on them. "I'm hardly recharged."

He sounded annoyed. "What's wrong with you? You losing steam already?"

"No—just exhausted. The drug causes major insomnia. Dr. Cole prescribed me Ambien to help, but the stuff makes me sleep cook. Yes, sleep cook. I woke up at the kitchen table with a bowl of mac and cheese in front of me."

He laughed.

"It's not funny, Tim. I could have burned the friggin' house down."

"Was it the microwave stuff?"

"Irrelevant. Point is, I'm exhausted. I need to sleep if I'm going to be of any use to you."

"Fine—get your sleep. Try Benadryl. It helps me. I'll call you if I hear anything."

I hung up without saying goodbye.

·　　·　　·

My cell rang an hour later. I snatched it and yelled: "*Tim!*"

His reply was flat. "We got another one."

CHAPTER 9

Morris had the decency to let me go back to sleep after elaborating, though I doubted I'd be able to after his grave curtness:

> *"It's our guy. Victim has all the hallmarks. Local PD is doing their thing. Get some sleep; we'll check it out first thing,"* he'd said.

·   ·   ·

I did manage to sleep. Some. No mac and cheese casualty this time, so I suppose that was good. When Morris picked me up, he wore a face I didn't approve of. It was the face of a man not grim for what we were about to see, but eager for what we were about to see. A chance for more leads, at the expense of lives.

"Definitely our guy," he said on the ride from Philly to Newark. "Everything matches." He then shot a casual glance out the driver's side window as though wishing the conversation immediately over. I caught it, though. Morris was king bluffer with everyone but me.

"What aren't you telling me?" I said.

He kept his eyes on the road as he spoke. "The body is badly burned."

"*Burned?*"

"Yeah. But the cuffs are there. The extreme ligature marks are there. Blunt-force trauma…"

"Right palm?"

"We'll see."

"Burned, huh?" I said.

"Yeah—burying didn't work, why not burn him this time?"

I couldn't tell whether he was being sarcastic.

"We were right," I said. "He didn't get what he wanted back in upstate Pennsylvania, so he went for another sooner than later."

"Much sooner. It could explain why he set him on fire. Lighting a match is a hell of a lot quicker than digging a hole."

I felt a flash of hope. "*Much* sooner," I repeated. "That means he might have screwed up."

Morris knew what I meant, but he wanted to think out loud. He said: "What do you mean?"

"No planning on this one," I said. "Much as it pains me to use your metaphor, he's got blue balls and needs to get his rocks off quick."

"Right. No more beauties to woo. It's last call—gotta take your pick from what's left in the place."

"Right."

"Our victim was opportunistic, not chosen," he said. "That means someone might have seen."

I nodded. "Good chance our bad guy left breadcrumbs he doesn't know about."

"Newark PD said the victim is homeless. Soup kitchen in Trenton confirmed this."

"*Trenton*? That's an hour south. How'd they put those pieces together so fast?"

"Same way everyone else does. Luck. The victim had been a regular face at the soup kitchen for years. Well liked. When he didn't show for days, a volunteer at the kitchen—she was close to the guy; Hal was his name—started making a fuss and was eventually heard. No easy task when it comes to missing homeless. Maybe we should bring her on board."

"And we're sure it's this Hal guy?"

Morris nodded. "Girl at the kitchen ID'd him this morning. Apparently it wasn't easy for her."

"It never is."

"No, I meant because of the condition the guy was in. He *literally* wasn't easy to identify."

"Oh."

"Yeah."

.   .   .

We rode in silence for a minute. I then said: "So the victim hunkered down in Trenton."

"Apparently."

"How'd he end up in Newark?"

"What our guy does requires privacy," Morris said.

"So maybe he lives in Newark?"

"My gut says no. For this one, he couldn't take his sweet old time. I mean, he *could*, but he couldn't—know what I mean?"

"Not even a little."

"Let me keep talking in metaphors."

"Just do it."

"His usual game is to find his date and bring her back to his place, so to speak. He was all set with the last one in upstate PA, but someone cock-blocks him."

I stifled a smirk. I can't encourage his speak, but I have to admit it does help me see the picture better sometimes, God help me. He continued.

"It's late; he doesn't have time to work on anyone else in particular. So he goes to a dive bar and starts looking for any hole with a heartbeat. He makes his catch, but doesn't have the time to take her back to his place for the privacy he wants. So he gets a room, so to speak, and does his absolute damnedest to make it feel like all the others."

"But...?"

"But it doesn't." Morris's face scrunched with uncertain thought. "That's why he sets this one on fire."

I frowned. "How does that work?"

"I don't know. Maybe..." Another uncertain scrunch. "Maybe..." He smacked the steering wheel with the base of his palm.

"Is this going to be a regular thing?" I asked.

"What?"

"You getting all tantrumy when you don't know what's what? You were never like this before."

He kept his eyes on the road and wouldn't afford me a glance. "I'm not a *total* dick, Mags. You think I would have contacted you if I wasn't desperate? Christ, your son died, your husband *just* died."

"You don't say."

CHAPTER 10

Newark, New Jersey

It was an abandoned textile mill. No great care had been taken to hide the body. Probably because no great care had been needed—even when the place was up and running I imagine employees got themselves lost from time to time. It was huge, with more corridors and doors taking you the wrong way than a liar would.

Local PD had found the body behind one of those wrong-way doors when a few homeless hunkering down in the mill for the night had noticed the smell. Not an ugly smell, they'd said, but a pleasant smell. A desirable smell.

"It smelled like *what*?" Morris asked Detective Brown, the lead homicide detective in charge.

"Barbecue," Detective Brown said. "Guys who found the body thought someone was grilling nearby—wandered on over to see whether they were feeling generous."

"Well, this is a first for me," Morris muttered.

"Not me," Brown said with a little smile, perhaps relishing his chance to one-up the sanctimonious Feds. "We found a guy cooked to a crisp in his toolshed a few years back. Meth lab fire. My wife and I were married in Maui, and we had the rehearsal dinner at a luau. We got to eat one of those giant pigs roasted over a spit. I'm telling ya, when they brought that guy's body out of his shed, it smelled exactly like that damn pig."

Morris didn't comment on the detective's pleasant little account.

Neither did I. Instead, I gestured down at the body and asked: "The guys who found him put out the fire?"

Detective Brown nodded. "Said he already looked dead—was just lying in here burning. They managed to toss a bunch of blankets on him and snuff out the flames, but he was already far gone. Blunt-force trauma is what killed him, though. Burning him after was just icing on the cake. We found an empty can of gasoline out there—" He gestured towards the door and the vast interior of the mill beyond. "Can looked kinda new. Besides, homeless know better than to start a campfire with gas. If it's from anyone, it's kids screwing around, or your guy. Must've brought it with him."

Morris snapped on a pair of gloves and squatted in front of the body. Local PD had extended the crime scene well beyond the room we occupied now, their efforts and chatter outside the room constant as they worked diligently. Brown closed the steel door in a bid to offer some quiet. The three of us now stood alone in the room with the body.

. . .

"Nobody heard any screaming or anything, just the smell," Brown said. He then looked around the airtight confines of the room. "Though I wonder whether they would have heard anything in here."

"They smelled something, though," I said.

Brown acknowledged my logic with a nod.

"Maybe gagged again?" I said to Morris, alluding to no screaming reported by the homeless who found him.

"Maybe," he said, still squatting and inspecting the body. "If so, it was likely burned away."

Brown looked confused. "You sure this is your guy?" he asked.

Morris didn't look up when he said: "Yes."

"Thought your guy just cuffed them and did a whack-a-mole job on their heads before he dumped them. Don't remember reading anything about setting them on fire. Think he was trying to cover his tracks?"

Morris finally stood. He ignored Brown's question, looked at me, and said: "Too burnt to get anything on the right palm."

"Right palm?" Brown said.

Still looking at me, Morris gestured to the shackle on the victim's ankle. "That's new."

"New but not significant, if you ask me," I said.

"How's that?" Morris said.

"I'd bet it's for restraint only. I can't see it serving a purpose for the fantasy."

Morris gestured down towards the cuffs that bound the victim's hands behind his back in trademark fashion. "He's got his restraint," he said. "Same as always. Why the leg iron too?"

I looked around the room. Four thick walls of concrete, a small window, and a steel door. No idea what purpose the room once served, but right now it reminded me of a prison cell—fine if your cellmate wasn't a bother; a nightmare if he was.

"This victim was different than the others," I said. "He's been living on the street his whole life, tough as nails. He wouldn't have been as compliant as the other victims were; there's no life-leverage to use against him should he threaten to fight back."

"Life-leverage?" Brown said.

"Sure," I said, turning to him. "You grab Dad and he'll do anything you tell him to if you threaten his wife and kids. Hell, most everyone has *some* kind of life-leverage."

"But not a homeless man," Brown said, catching on.

"Right. The only life-leverage a man like that has is his life, and that's very little. The hardships and dangers they face every day? They'd laugh at the threat of their own life as a means of manipulation."

"Manipulation for what? What's he do with them?" Brown asked.

I shrugged. "We haven't gotten that far yet. Point is, the leg iron was used as a fail-safe, in case our victim decided to fight."

"But he was cuffed from behind too," Brown said.

Morris finally joined in. "A fellow agent—" He stopped and looked at me. "You know Agent Holt."

I nodded.

"A fellow agent was headbutted unconscious while their suspect was cuffed from behind. Then the suspect dove headfirst into Holt's partner—" He paused and looked at me again. "Becker."

I nodded again.

"Then the suspect dove headfirst into Agent Becker's waist with all the force of a linebacker, knocking him on his ass without a breath of air. Suspect managed a good distance before Agent Becker was able to catch up to him. Holt's nose is still crooked."

Holt had once told me he got his trademark nose in a bar fight with three guys. I was eager to see him again.

"Why did you ask about the right palm?" Brown said.

Morris looked confused for a moment. It was an act. "Huh? Oh, that was nothing—just talking out loud."

Brown seemed to buy it. "Gotcha. Anything else I can get you guys?"

"Few minutes alone would be great, Detective." Morris gave a genuine smile.

Brown frowned. "Alone?"

"Please."

"What for?" He aimed the file in his hand at the victim and then brandished it. "Anything else you wanna know about this guy is in here."

Morris smiled again. "Oh, I know that; I wasn't suggesting otherwise. Just a few minutes."

Both Detective Brown and his frown stayed put.

Morris stopped smiling. "Please." He was no longer asking.

Brown sucked his teeth and flashed a contemptuous smile. "Sure thing." He then raised the file again. "Should I even offer it?"

"That would be really helpful, thank you," Morris said.

Detective Brown handed the file over to me while keeping his eyes on Morris. He turned and left without another word.

·　　·　　·

"So what happened to being all chummy and greasing the wheels with local PD?" I said.

"I thought I was fine," Morris said.

"Why'd you hold back the right palm detail? You worried about leaks?"

"Yeah. The right palm has been the one detail we've been able to keep away from the media. I'd like to keep it that way."

"By saying it in front of him?"

"I got lost for a moment. It was dumb."

"Yeah it was."

His ice-blue eyes clicked on me, his expression void of our usual levity. "I got lost for a moment. It was dumb," he said again.

"Okay…" I said with a polite, if not patronizing, little smile. "So what do we have here?"

"We have a homeless man, likely abducted from Trenton."

"His dive-bar girl after being cock-blocked in upstate Pennsylvania," I said, hoping my using one of his metaphors might ease his weird intensity.

"Right."

"How'd he get him in the car?" I asked.

"Money's always good."

"Soup kitchen girl said he'd been on the street for years. He'd be wary of cars flashing money."

"Unless he turned tricks," he said.

"Did he?"

"No idea."

"Let's say he didn't. Car rolls up and offers money. Guy that street savvy isn't just going to climb into a car for the promise of money."

"Never underestimate the power of the almighty dollar," he said.

"Okay, let's run with that then. He promises a ton of cash. For what?"

"Does it matter?" he asked.

"Sure it does—how'd our guy get the victim to agree to go all the way from Trenton to Newark?"

"Maybe the victim didn't think he was *going* to Newark."

"So then where did he think he was going?"

Morris leapt ahead. "Why burn him?"

"Wait, wait, wait," I said. "Let's back up a minute."

"No," Morris insisted, pulling a roll of TUMS from his pocket and popping a few. "Let's do the here and now. Why'd he burn him?"

"We can only arrive at the here and now if we go back to the *then* and *before*."

"Bullshit—we *are* here. Why'd he burn him?"

"You know what I mean. The only way we're going to understand this man is if we reconstruct his methodology."

"Are you really going to stand there and lecture me?"

"Your seniority doesn't make you impervious to impulsiveness, Tim. I know the heat you're getting. You asked for my help—let me help you."

"So then help me," he said. "Do your thing."

I'd taken the drug on the ride from Philly to Newark. It'd had more than enough time to kick in by now, but as I'd mentioned before, I had no way of knowing when it would do its thing, or whether it would even happen at all. Simply willing my senses to get all uber-receptive didn't work. Whenever it happened, it came on with the suddenness, and momentarily helplessness, of a sneeze. Right now the only thing I sensed, maybe a bit stronger than usual, was the smell of peppermint from the TUMS Morris had just finished munching.

"It'll happen when it happens," I said. "In the meantime, there's this thing called investigating that has proved to be pretty successful over the years."

Morris made a weird grumbly noise in his throat—brat for "fine."

"Thank you," I said with a smidge of condescending calm. "Let's backtrack a little then. If our victim didn't know he was going from Trenton to Newark, where did he think he was going? What would keep you in the car for all that distance?"

"I still say money," Morris said. "Street savvy or not, money changes things."

He was right. Money was capable of disturbing feats.

"All right, let's say money got him to Newark," I said. "What then? What got him in here?" I waved my arm around the room. "What got him in those?" I pointed to the leg iron and the cuffs. "No way money did that. And remember, our guy has no life-leverage on the victim."

"There had to be *some* kind of leverage. Either that or the victim was unconscious when he was cuffed and shackled."

I opened the file and started reading. Head still in the file, I pointed to the west wall where local PD had lifted prints. "Local PD lifted several prints there." I then pointed to the far wall. "And there."

"I know," he said, sounding dejected. "They're the victim's prints."

I lifted my head from the file. "You're missing the point. If the victim's prints are on two of the four walls, that means he wasn't cuffed at the time. How could he have been?" I motioned down at the victim and the way he was cuffed behind his back like all the others.

Morris's dejected face started to come to life. "Go on."

"How do you get cuffs on a man with nothing to lose?"

"You threaten him."

I snorted. "With what? There's no daddy with a family here. This was a man who went to sleep every night prepared for it to be his last."

Morris looked dejected again.

I handed the file to Morris and glanced back at the far wall. "How many prints did they lift from here?"

Morris scanned the file. "A lot," he eventually said.

"And the west wall?"

He dropped his head into the file again. "Quite a few on that one too."

"Both hands?"

He groaned and read some more. "Yeah."

"Weird."

"What?"

"Why *both* hands? He couldn't have been testing for give—it's concrete."

"Maybe he was pounding on the wall? Calling for help?"

"Who pounds on a concrete wall?"

"Someone who's desperate. Scared shitless."

"What scares the shit out of a hardened man like our victim?"

There was a hard and fast knock on the door. Detective Brown entered before we told him to. "Thought you two should know," he said. "We just got word from Trenton PD. They got a witness."

CHAPTER 11

Trenton, New Jersey

Our witness turned out to be another homeless. A black man by the name of Reggie Boyle who claimed to be a good friend of Hal's.

"And you're sure the make of the car was a Toyota?" Morris asked.

Reggie Boyle nodded emphatically, almost childlike in his certainty. "A Toyota, yup. It was a Toyota, I seen it."

"But you don't remember the model," Morris said.

The emphatic child left Reggie's face. He dropped his head. "No...couldn't make it out." His head suddenly popped up, the eager child back, hoping to offer consolation. "It was silver, though! Or gray...gray or silver...gray or silver Toyota...gray or silver."

"You say you got a look at the driver?" I said.

Reggie nodded. "I seen him. White boy."

"What else?" Morris said.

Reggie shrugged. "Looked like a white boy. All y'all look alike."

"Hal was white," I said.

Reggie smiled. "All *y'all* white folks look alike."

Morris started to ask another question when Reggie suddenly blurted: "*Hold up!* Why'd you just say 'was'? Hal *was* white? He dead?"

"Yes, I'm sorry," Morris said.

Reggie spun away from us and stomped the ground. When he turned back, he had tears in his eyes. "How'd he die?"

"That's not important right now, Mr. Boyle," Morris said. "But we'd like you to try to remember—"

"It's important to *me*. How'd he die?"

"He was murdered," Morris said evenly.

"White boy who picked him up do it?"

"We don't know."

Reggie spun and stomped again, cursing this time.

"Mr. Boyle, can you please try to remember more about the man's appearance? It may help us find him."

Reggie turned back. "I don't know...looked like you, I guess," he said, waving a hand up and down Morris.

I glanced at Morris and then back at Reggie. "He had dark hair? Blue eyes?"

"Dark hair, yeah. Couldn't see his eyes too good."

"Anything else?" I asked. "I know he was in a car, but...anything else you can remember? Did he appear fat? Skinny?"

Reggie shrugged, still visibly upset by the news about Hal. "I don't know—kinda average, I guess."

Of course he was. I'm still waiting for the day when a serial killer looks anything *but* average.

"Y'all say Hal was murdered?" Reggie said.

Morris only nodded.

"How?"

"I'd rather not get into it, Mr. Boyle," Morris said, reaching into his pocket for his TUMS. He popped a few and immediately began crunching them. The smell of peppermint was brutally strong—strong enough to make me spin away from both men as though they'd offended me.

"Maggie?" Morris said to my back.

Apparently sense of smell is closely linked with memory, more so than any of our other senses. This was something I recollected only in hindsight. At that exact moment, no such recollection was forthcoming. Instead, the world went away again, just as it had at the crime scene in upstate PA.

The drug was doing its thing again, and I found myself transported back to Newark, in the concrete room with Hal at our feet, horribly burned, Morris impatient, wanting to skip ahead, insistent on knowing why this particular victim had been burned:

> *"Why burn him?" Morris.*
> *"Wait, wait, wait—let's back up a minute." Me.*
> *"No." Morris goes into his pocket, pulls the roll of peppermint TUMS, pops a few into his mouth. "Let's do the here and now. Why'd he burn him?"*

Quick fast-forward to a moment later:

> *"How do you get cuffs on a man with nothing to lose?" Me.*
> *"You threaten him." Morris.*
> *"With what? There's no daddy with a family here. This was a man who went to sleep every night prepared for it to be his last."*

A second quick fast-forward:

> *"Maybe he was pounding on the wall? Calling for help?"*
> *"Who pounds on a concrete wall?"*
> *"Someone who's desperate. Scared shitless."*
> *"What scares the shit out of a hardened man like our victim?"*

A quick rewind now as something begins to gel.

> *"Why'd he burn him?"*

.   .   .

The world came back, the concrete room in Newark gone as suddenly as a dream upon waking.

I immediately spun back and looked straight into Reggie's eyes. "He was burned, Reggie. Set on fire. Who would do that, you think? Who would burn him?"

Morris's face dropped in disbelief at what I'd just blurted.

Reggie's face was far different. It was neither the sad nor angry it had been volleying between since our visit, but now ashen and disturbed.

"Oh man…" Reggie said. "Oh man, that's bad…oh man, that's really bad…"

"Why is that bad, Reggie?" I asked. "Why is that *really* bad?"

Reggie looked at me with the face of a child again. A frightened child. "Hal's afraid of fire. I mean really afraid, like a man who's afraid of snakes and spiders, you know? He don't even smoke, he's so afraid."

"Why is he afraid of fire?" I asked.

"Y'all remember that crazy-ass white boy who was coming into the projects, settin' fire to all of us? Trying to 'clean up' the streets? This about ten years back."

I didn't, but Morris apparently did. "I remember," he said.

Reggie nodded. "Yeah, well, Hal was one he tried to burn. I didn't know him then. Obviously Hal lived, but when some crazy-ass cracker pours gasoline all over you while you're trying to sleep, it's gonna stay with you, you know what I'm saying? Like I said, Hal won't even smoke—" He suddenly rubbed at his eyes, trying to stop the tears before they arrived. "Now he ain't *ever* gonna smoke, is he?"

"Mr. Boyle," Morris began, "we're going to have a few more questions for you, okay? Right now I'd like a few minutes to talk with my colleague. That all right?"

Reggie nodded and walked away, head down. He leaned back against one of the alley walls and slid down onto his butt. He started to light a cigarette, considered the match, and then angrily tossed both the cigarette and the match away. He pulled a pint bottle of whiskey from his coat, took a big swig, tucked it away again, and then dropped his head between his knees and started to cry.

.　　.　　.

Morris spun on me. "What the hell was that?"

"What?"

"I had no intention of telling him this victim had been burned."

"I know; that's why I did."

He shook his head, annoyed. "That was careless, Maggie."

Maggie, not Mags, again. Such melodrama made my brain hurt.

"Oh, come on, you think the homeless are going to spring a leak?" I said. "I'm surprised they were willing to speak to *us*."

"We would have eventually linked the victim to the fire incident from ten years ago."

"I did it sooner," I said. "Isn't that why I'm here?"

Morris sighed. "Why'd you blurt it out like that? Turn away from us and all? You have one of your things?"

I nodded. "I think so. The peppermint smell of your TUMS triggered it. You were chewing them back in Trenton when you kept insisting on knowing why this one had been burned. You started chewing them here, I got a whiff, and suddenly it was like I was in a kooky time machine, back to a few hours ago when we were looking at Hal's body."

Morris still looked annoyed. "So then what, you needed the smell of peppermint to help you remember something I'd said from only a few hours ago?"

"No—but the clarity of the memory was stronger than anything I'd ever experienced before in my life. Running it all back like that...it was like watching a film for the second time and seeing it in a different light."

"*Different light*? What the hell is that supposed to mean?"

"I don't know. Just that it had more impact the second time around. Either way, it wasn't a bad thing, was it?"

Morris threw up a hand. "So do I just keep on chewing TUMS until we catch him, is that it?"

I couldn't hide my frustration. "You just admitted you weren't planning on telling Reggie about the victim being burned, right? Well, I *did* tell him, and look what it got us."

"What?" Morris said. "What did it get us? Please enlighten me."

"We know how our guy got cuffs on a man with nothing to lose. We know what makes a hardened man like the victim desperate enough to pound on concrete walls."

"Fire."

I shook my head. "Fire was the conduit."

"His *fear* of fire then," Morris said.

"Exactly."

"So you think our guy exploited the victim's fear of fire to get him to do what he wanted."

"At some point, yes."

"He still bashed him in the head though. That's what actually killed him, not the fire."

"The fire seemed more significant to me," I said. "It's why I told Reggie it was the cause of death."

Morris started gnawing his thumbnail in thought.

"Again," I said, "the fire—or the *fear* of fire—was just a tool to help fulfill the fantasy."

Morris stopped eating his thumb. "This was a one-night stand, remember? You don't even know the *name* of a one-night stand. How the hell could our guy have known the victim was so afraid of fire?"

"I don't know. Could have come up in conversation. Reggie said he spotted the victim willingly get into the car. It could have been all buddy-buddy for a while as they drove north."

"You mean like, 'How 'bout them Yankees, oh, and what scares the shit out of you?'"

"Would you stop?"

Morris glanced over at Reggie. Reggie hadn't moved. I saw remorse in Morris's eyes. He turned back to me. "Let's let local PD finish questioning Reggie. I say you and I hole up for the night and fine-comb everything we've gotten so far." He then went into his pocket and handed me his roll of TUMS. "For inspiration," he said.

I gave him a look and started towards the car.

CHAPTER 12

Morris and I found a Comfort Inn in Morrisville (I thought he was joking at first, but that really was the name of the town), Pennsylvania, about fifteen minutes from the alley in Trenton where the seventh victim had been abducted. The motel was utilitarian and clean, and I was grateful. A hot shower until I was pink and pruned superseded all else as far as I was concerned.

Morris apparently didn't get that memo; I was no sooner stepping into the shower when he came knocking. I wrapped a towel around my head and torso and went to the door. The bulbous view from the peephole made his receding hairline appear larger than life. I snickered and let him in.

"What's funny?" he said.

"Maybe we pick up some Rogaine later?"

He frowned and ran a hand through his thinning hair. "I blame the job."

"Blame your parents. What do you want?"

"I could use a drink," he said.

"What happened to 'holing up' and 'fine-combing' everything?"

"Yes or no?" he said.

I groaned. "Give me a minute."

I went into the bathroom and changed. I glanced longingly at the shower before exiting and said: "I *will* see you again."

.   .   .

I was on my second glass of chardonnay and feeling mellow. Drinking on the drug—along with the other drugs I was using to combat *the* drug's side effects—was contraindicated, of course. Not long after Christopher passed, I put away more than half a bottle of vodka on a stomach full of the drug and nothing else; I hadn't eaten in days.

Maybe it was the drinking on an exceptionally empty stomach—it surely didn't help—or maybe it was mixing that much booze with the drug—almost assuredly the culprit; that much booze with cough drops was just plain dumb—but I ended up in the ER with a reaction that went well beyond mere alcohol poisoning. The best way I could describe it would be like having a soul-punishing case of the flu. Hot and gross and bad and everything coming in relentless waves. Ironically (and it wasn't even Irony Appreciation Day!), being that sick took my mind off Christopher for bits at a time.

That was until the dreams came.

Bad flu often comes with bad dreams. Fever dreams. When it all seems so real, yet so impossible. Christopher would visit me in these dreams. He would look like he did when he was healthy…and then he would look like he did days before he died, always asking me for help, wondering why I'd allowed this to happen to him. I would tell myself it was a dream, *know* it was a dream, yet my body would always betray me, insist I lie there paralyzed, in my real bed, in my real bedroom, and watch the unreal image of my dead son asking me for help.

I wouldn't even wish such a thing on the drunken asshole who ended up killing my husband.

.   .   .

So then why the *hell* was I having a drink now, you ask? Well, a glass or two of chardonnay isn't half a bottle or more of vodka, is it? Plus, I'd be lying if I said I hadn't touched a drop since the ER incident; I mentioned I'd had a glass of wine with Morris in Philadelphia.

Wine was my alternative to benzodiazepines—drugs like Xanax and Klonopin and Valium. I'd had my fair share of benzos in the past under Dr. Cole's care, and while they certainly helped at times, I didn't feel they were crucial, especially considering the myriad other drugs I was ingesting, least of all *the* drug. A glass or two of wine mellowed me out just as much as popping a pill of Xanax did, plus I was getting all the additional benefits of those antioxidants found in wine, wasn't I? Perhaps I'll use that one again when *Enabling Yourself Appreciation Day* rolls around.

Seriously, though, it'd been long enough to where I knew my limits now. I never ventured further than two glasses of wine, even on a full stomach.

.   .   .

It was around eight o'clock when Morris and I returned to the motel. We retired to our separate rooms, and I immediately went for the shower I was forced to leave waiting. "Hello, handsome. Miss me?" I adjusted the temperature. "What do you say we get it nice and hot, hmmm?"

Sadly, this was the closest I'd come to dirty talk in a long time.

.   .   .

Showered and wrapped in towels, still feeling mellow from the wine, I lay down on the bed and recapped everything Morris and I had covered at the bar...

"So he picks him up," Morris said. "How?"

"You like the money angle," I said.

"I do."

"All right then, he offers him money. But for what?"

"Huh?"

"Reggie said he was an average-looking white guy. So an average-looking white guy cruises by an alley in a rough neighborhood and just randomly offers a homeless man some money, provided he gets into his car and goes for a ride? No way. There has to be more of an incentive."

"Money is the king of all incentives, especially if you don't have any."

I shook my head. "You're missing the point. He's not just giving him the money; he's doing it on the condition that the victim gets into the car. What's the condition?"

Morris sipped his scotch. "Maybe he's lost. Like you said, an average-looking white guy in a rough neighborhood—maybe he says he's lost, needs help finding his way out."

"And he doesn't want mere directions," I added, "he wants someone *in* the car with him, showing him the way. He's offering money, after all."

Morris started nodding. "Okay...okay, good—let's stick with that for now."

"All right. So we know they ended up in Newark. Maybe our guy tells the victim he lives there?"

"Right." He started crunching on some ice. "But once the victim gets our guy going in the right direction, he'll want out, right? Why would he want to venture an hour north from his 'home,' so to speak?"

"Our guy knew the victim was afraid of fire. Maybe he threatened to burn him if he didn't stay put."

Morris frowned. "How the hell do you burn a guy while driving? Without putting yourself in danger, no less?"

"Well, he wouldn't actually burn him in the car, of course; but he could still make the threat."

"And if our victim was as scared shitless of fire as Reggie said, what would stop him from jumping out of a moving car after such a threat was made?"

"Locked doors."

"And what would stop him from putting up a fight? Grabbing the wheel and running them off the road, anything to avoid being burned?"

I sipped my wine and said nothing. Morris was right; even in a movie, the idea of the bad guy threatening to burn the victim in the car while he was driving would have caused eye-rolling and groans.

"So can we rule out a threat then?" Morris asked. "Keeping the victim's butt in the car for an hour-long drive from Trenton to Newark, can we rule out a threat?"

"I think so," I said. "The victim doesn't seem the type to respond to threats, and the one possible exception of fire just doesn't work."

"So he went willingly."

I thought about that. It was the only other alternative, wasn't it? I sipped the last of my second glass of wine and sat back in my chair with a long sigh, savoring the calming effect the wine was beginning to have on my mind and body.

I thought about when Mike and I used to stay in on a Saturday night before Christopher was born. We would get takeout and drink lots of wine and giggle and fool around, even role-play; the wine always lowered our inhibitions and made us naughty.

Before Christopher had been diagnosed, we really did have it good, Mike and I. Once Christopher had been diagnosed and especially after he'd left us, I found it impossible to move on, and Mike had grown increasingly frustrated with my inability to do so. I often wondered, if Mike hadn't died, *would* we have eventually moved on? Could we have toughed it out, or, more precisely, could *I* have toughed it out?

Mike is dead.

I never needed a reminder about my son, but I often—for reasons I truly didn't know—forgot that my husband was gone. Maybe it was because things had gotten so bad between us, right up until the very end?

My husband is dead. Like Christopher. Both of them dead.

I stood from the table. "I'm going to get another glass of wine. You want anything?"

I expected him to object to my third glass of wine, but then I'd never told him about my two-drink limit. He was my partner, and we were close, but he wasn't Dr. Cole. Besides, I'd felt it was all ultimately irrelevant anyway as I had no such intentions of imbibing on the drug ever again—

(except now, right?)

(I'm sad; I need it)

(so Enabling Yourself Appreciation Day has arrived in full swing, has it?)

—and so instead of objecting, Morris merely pointed to his scotch glass and said: "Same again, please."

.   .   .

I went to the bar and ordered our drinks.

"Hey, Red...haven't seen you around here before."

I turned and faced a guy who looked like he paid rent for the barstool on which his fat butt was plopped. And "Red?" *Really?*

"That's because I'm not from around here," I said.

"Damn shame. Can I interest you in a tour guide?" A lecherous smirk followed his offer.

"No, you cannot."

"Come on, Red, I won't bite...maybe." A bump of the eyebrows above the lecherous smirk now.

I was more fascinated by the guy than I was repulsed. Well, I was repulsed, but still, I hadn't thought guys like this existed. He was a real-life cliché that seemed to have wandered out of a film. I wondered whether he ever picked up a woman looking and acting the way he did, and if so, what the hell were *they* like? Still, fascinated or not, he needed some place-putting, and I was happy to do it.

"If you did bite, it would be considered assault. And, being a federal agent, I would then be justified in shooting you in the dick."

Cliché spun his fat back to me and said no more. That cheered me up a bit.

.   .   .

I returned to our table and handed Morris his scotch.

"Thanks," he said after taking a healthy sip. "I think I'm done after this one. Any more and I'll be snoozing right here—" He tapped his index finger on our table.

I took my own healthy sip of my chardonnay and considered Morris's words...

Which made me think about Mike and I becoming uninhibited after too much wine...

Which made me sad and want to take another sip...

Which made me think about Reggie mourning the victim and going for the whiskey in his pocket to ease the pain...

Which brought me back to Morris saying any more scotch and he'd be snoozing right here at the table...

Which made me suddenly lean into the table, eager for Morris's ear.

"He drugged him," I said excitedly. "Our guy *drugged* the victim."

Now Morris leaned in. We looked like we were planning a heist of some kind. "Drugged him how?"

"It's going to sound way stereotypical—homeless guy helpless to alcohol—but I think our guy offered the victim booze. The booze was drugged."

"Why?"

"Reggie smelled like whiskey. And when we let him go, he immediately tucked into a pint of booze. Reggie and the victim were best friends. The victim was too afraid of fire to smoke—and who can blame him—but who's to say he stayed away from booze?"

"So the victim gets in the car and our guy offers him a drink?" Morris said.

"Why not? It's like an icebreaker of sorts."

"Would a cagey man like the victim accept booze from a stranger?"

"Perhaps. What if the victim was a drinker? I mean a big drinker. It's his vice. We know Reggie had a bottle at the ready..."

"All right, I'll buy this," Morris said. "So our guy offers the victim a drink or two during the drive, and the victim accepts, not knowing that our guy slipped him a big mickey."

I nodded. "The victim passes out in the passenger seat, and now our guy is free to take him anywhere he wants without bother."

"So he takes him to the abandoned mill in Newark and shackles him by the ankle."

"Right."

"Then what?"

I frowned. "Then what?"

"Yeah."

"Well, if we knew that, we wouldn't be—"

"No, I don't mean *that* 'then what?' I mean…then what?"

I splayed a hand. "You lost me, Tim."

"I mean, did he burn him, then whack him? Whack him, then burn him? Both? What about trophies? You still thinking he took photos or maybe filmed it? What about the right palm?"

My splayed hand became a stop hand. "Whoa, slow it down a little, please."

He cocked his head and eyed me curiously. "Having trouble keeping up?"

"When you become Alex Trebek on Red Bull I do. Give me one at a time."

He crunched a big hunk of ice, probably wishing it was my head. "Okay, the victim wakes up in the concrete room we found him in. He's shackled and disoriented. Did anyone see our guy taking the victim inside the mill? Inside the concrete room? If the victim was unconscious, our guy had to be carrying or dragging him."

"Homeless squatting in the mill smelled the burning body; it's what got them curious," I said.

Morris made an unpleasant face. "Right—*barbecue*."

"Point is, they only checked it out *after* smelling barbecue," I said. "If they'd seen something shady prior to that, they probably would have fled. Their whole existence relies on self-preservation, looking the other way."

"They did try to save the victim, putting out the fire," he said.

"They did, yes."

"So maybe they didn't look the other way this time."

"Except Newark PD questioned them and got nothing," I said.

"Right…" Morris took a big sip and began sucking on a piece of ice this time, no crunch.

We were stuck. Everything up until now had strong retail value, but from here on out, we were struggling to sell anything.

"Shackled in the concrete room," I said.

"Yeah."

"He's unconscious from the drugged booze," I said.

"Assuming that's what he did."

"Why not cuff him then? Why wait until he's awake to get the cuffs on him? The fingerprints all over two of the four walls told us our guy didn't cuff the victim until he was conscious."

"Maybe he woke up."

I sipped my wine. It *was* the simplest explanation. Or...

"Maybe it's not part of the fantasy," I said.

"Cuffing is part of the fantasy? Explain that."

"I can't—not yet."

"What *can* we explain about his methodology? What drives him?"

I sipped more wine as my mind churned. "Exploiting the victim's fear of fire can't be a coincidence; there has to be a connection there."

Morris spat the piece of ice he'd been sucking back into his glass. "If you'd told me our guy had been following the victim months—even weeks—out, then maybe I'd buy it. But this victim was a one-night stand, remember? There's simply no way he could have known about the victim's fear of fire beforehand, much less planned on utilizing it somehow."

"If the victim was indeed drugged, he might have mentioned his fear of fire to our guy without even realizing," I said.

"Okay, fine—I'll buy that. But my point still stands. No way our guy could have been depending on such a thing. It was a fluke. A—forgive me for saying—pleasant bonus for our guy to have such an exploitable fear divulged to him."

"Unless our guy simply asked him," I said.

Morris drained his scotch. "Asked him if he was afraid of *fire*? Pretty random."

"How about just asked him what he was afraid of?"

"Reggie said the victim's fear of fire was so intense he was even afraid to smoke. Why would he offer up such a phobia to a complete stranger?"

"Because he was drugged," I said with some satisfaction. Though I'm not sure why. To dust off an old chestnut, it felt like we really had only just scratched the surface.

"All right," Morris said. "Our guy simply asked, and the victim, in his drugged state, told him. There's our guy's leverage to do whatever the hell he does with them before bashing their heads in. No life-leverage like the other victims, so there's our guy's leverage on *this* victim: find out what scares the hell out of him and threaten to make it happen."

"Right," I said. "And gasoline and a basic igniter aren't exactly difficult items to come by at the last minute—our guy could have picked them up while the victim was shackled and unconscious in the mill."

"Right," Morris said. "Good thing for our guy the victim wasn't afraid of sharks."

"Funny."

. . .

We sat quiet for a moment, digesting it all.

"Okay then," he eventually said.

"Okay then," I said.

Another moment of silence. We then exchanged a look as though neither of us had studied for the test, yet were offering to copy off one another.

Morris eventually let out a long sigh and ran both hands down his face. "There's so much more."

"Yeah…" I finished the last of my wine. "Maybe we should call it a night."

Morris gave a tired nod and stood. "I'll go settle the tab."

. . .

And so now, showered and wrapped in towels and lying on the motel bed, still mellow from wine, having gone over everything Morris and I covered at the bar, I recalled Dr. Cole's words about my not needing the drug to sharpen my investigative skills. I recalled telling him I needed the drug to expedite, not sharpen.

I still believe that.

Now, if I could only expedite things to the next level and get a solid peek into this whacko's mind, his methodology, I just might be able to start tapering my dose of the drug back to that therapeutic and less harmful range again.

Assuming I still cared about living.

CHAPTER 13

Joe Pierce walked into the camera shop right before closing. Born Jody Pierce, he'd insisted on Joe for over a decade now. Jody was a pussy name, a girl's name.

The young male employee behind the counter greeted him with a chummy smile. "Hey, man, how can I help you?"

"I was in here a few months back. I bought an infrared camera."

"Oh right! I remember now. How'd it work out for you?"

"Good. Only got to use it once though. Next trip was kinda... cancelled last minute."

"Ah geez, that sucks. What can I help you with today?"

"I'm interested in a headcam."

"Oh yeah? For anything in particular?"

"Spelunking," Joe lied. "For caves."

"No shit?" The young man quickly slapped a hand over his mouth and looked around the store. No one was there. He giggled and said: "Pardon my French. *Spelunking*, huh? You got bigger balls than I do, bro."

Joe cocked his head. "What do you mean?"

"Digging around in caves? Eff *that*."

"You're afraid of caves?" Joe asked.

"*Hell* yeah, man. Imagine if one of those things came crumbling down on you? Buried you alive?" He performed an exaggerated shudder. "*Brrrr!*"

Joe Pierce looked suddenly repulsed. "You're a grown man," he said. "How can you be afraid of something? Something a *girl* would be afraid of?"

The young man took a step back from the counter. "I was just saying, man."

"So you're afraid of being buried alive, is that it?" Joe asked.

The young man had no more room to back up. He started sliding to the left of the glass counter. "Yeah, I guess I am," he said.

Joe started laughing.

Nervous reflex soon had the young man laughing too. "What's so funny?" he asked.

"Just an amazing coincidence is all," Joe said. "Can you show me what you have now?"

CHAPTER 14

I'd only just closed my eyes when there was yet another knock on my motel room door. I rolled out of bed and began cursing Morris under my breath as I dressed.

I looked through the peephole, and there he was, receding hair-line as prominent as ever through the funhouse lens. I decided to skip the Rogaine joke this time and just open the door and give him crap for waking me.

"You know, a phone call works just as well," I said as I opened the door.

Morris wasn't there.

I poked my head outside, looked left and right down the line of motel doors. "Tim?"

He wasn't there.

I looked farther out, towards the rows of cars in the motel's lot. Was he hiding among them, playing a stupid game?

"Tim?"

My peripheral vision caught something in the distance. A man, walking away from the lot, heading east towards the strip of road that separated the motel from a field beyond. The man was mostly silhouetted by streetlamps and the motel sign, but it looked like Morris.

"*Tim?*" I called.

The man didn't turn around, just kept on going, looking as if he meant to cross the street and venture into the field.

"Is he sleepwalking?" I said to myself. Then, to the man in the distance again: "*Tim Morris!*"

Still, he didn't turn around.

Maybe it's not Morris, I thought.

Well, it was definitely Morris looking into your peephole just now.

True. So then where the hell did he go?

Out by the road. The man in the distance is Morris.

How could he have gotten from my peephole to the road so fast?

Logic was buying into time. If that was indeed Morris in the distance, sleepwalking and about to cross the street, he could be in danger.

I went back into the room, grabbed my hotel key, my jacket, and a pair of shoes, and started after—

Stop.

What?

Check his room first. If he's there, you know the guy by the road isn't Morris.

I knocked on Morris's door. "Tim? Open up, it's me."

I waited, periodically glancing over my shoulder at the man in the distance. He was stopped by the edge of the road now, as if he was uncertain about whether he wanted to cross.

Would a sleepwalker do that? Look both ways?

I knocked again, harder now. "*Tim?* Tim, open up, it's me."

"*Mags?*"

"Yeah—open up."

The motel door opened. Morris stood there in boxer shorts and a tee, disheveled, sleep in his eyes. "What is it?"

I opened my mouth, only to close it again without a word. I didn't even know where to begin.

"You all right?" Morris asked. "What's wrong?"

I looked over my shoulder towards the street again.

The man was gone.

I spun back to Morris. "You were just at my door," I said. "I saw you. You were *just* at my door."

Morris rubbed at one of his eyes with a palm. "You were dreaming, Mags. I promise you, I've been asleep ever since we parted ways earlier."

"I *saw* you." I looked over my shoulder once again. The man was still gone. "And then out there..." I pointed east towards the street and the field beyond. "I mean, I think it was you. It *was* you...I think."

Morris leaned his torso out the door and looked east. He then pulled it back inside, his tired face now growing concerned. "Mags, listen to yourself—what you're saying doesn't make any sense. You were dreaming, that's all."

"No, I was—"

"You had three glasses of wine tonight," he said. "Two's your limit when taking a full dose of the drug. Any more gives you bad dreams. Do the math."

I did the math.

Morris's result was sound; mine was not.

I *did* have three glasses of wine tonight instead of my usual two. The gravity of my life had unexpectedly emerged from its pit of suppression, and I'd foolishly felt that a third glass was the weight needed to push it back down.

One last glance over my shoulder.

No man by the road.

I turned back to Morris and found it tough to look him in the eye.

"Okay, fine," I said. "I was dreaming. Sorry I woke you." I turned and started back to my room.

"You gonna be okay?" he called after me.

I reached my door and gave a half-hearted nod in his direction.

·　　·　　·

I went back inside my room, closed my eyes, and leaned my forehead against the door, letting out a long, frustrated sigh.

"*You had three glasses of wine tonight,*" Morris said. "*Two's your limit when taking a full dose of the drug. Any more gives you bad dreams. Do the math.*"

I did the math again.

This time it didn't add up.

I'd never told Morris about the interaction between alcohol and the drug.

My two-drink limit.

The bad dreams.

I'd never told him because his plate was plenty full as it was without heaping my personal bullshit on top of it all.

I'd never told him because I thought it would be irrelevant—I never figured I'd be stupid enough to drink too much on the drug ever again.

I'd never told him. Period.

I spun and opened the door, hurried back towards Morris's room, keen on getting an explanation. I hoped for his sake (and mine, *especially* mine) that the explanation was damn good.

CHAPTER 15

I was not courteous this time when knocking on Morris's door. Didn't even use my knuckles, but the bottom of my fist like a hammer: *Whump! Whump! Whump!*

"Tim! Tim, open up!"

Nothing.

"*Tim!*" *Whump! Whump! Whump!*

I pressed my ear to the door, hoping to hear him grumbling some kind of reply as he fumbled for the light.

I heard nothing.

"*TIM!*" *Whump! Whump! Whump! Whump! Whump!*

"*Can I help you?*"

I spun and found an annoyed-looking man staring at me. I recognized him almost immediately as the motel manager who had checked us in.

"I'm a federal agent," I said. "You checked us in, remember? My partner isn't answering the door. I'm worried something might be wrong. Would you please open it for me?"

The motel manager sighed. "Ma'am, please just go back to your room and sleep it off—I don't want any trouble."

I nearly stuttered. "*What?* Did you *hear* me? I am no longer asking but *ordering* you to open this door. *Now.*"

The manager gave another sigh and started towards Morris's door.

"*Thank you*," I said condescendingly. It was all I could do to keep from punching him in the throat.

The manager slid his master key into the lock and opened Morris's door. I stepped inside the dark room and immediately patted the wall for the lights.

The room lit up, and my mouth fell open.

The bed was made; the room was tidy. *Maid*-tidy. As if no one had ever been there.

"Happy?" the motel manager said behind me.

My head was spinning.

Dreaming…I'm dreaming again.

"No," I whispered to myself. "No, I'm not."

Wrong room…it has to be the wrong room.

I spun and checked the door. Its digits read room 316.

"What the…?" I muttered. I tapped a finger against the number and looked back at the manager. "This is wrong. This number is *wrong*."

"Ma'am, there's no one currently occupying this room."

I shook my head. "No, no, this room number, it—Morris is in 12, I'm in 11…"

The manager looked on the verge of raising his voice. "Ma'am, please just go and—"

"*316?*" I blurted. "How many rooms do you *have*?" I shoved the manager aside and all but ran back to my room. The room number on my door was now 914. "What the *hell*?!"

I turned back to the manager. He was gone.

"*Hello!?*"

I ran back to Morris's room. The door was closed. The room number was 12 again.

I ran back to my room. The room number was 11 again.

"I'm dreaming," I said again. "I *have* to be."

Why were the room numbers 316 and 914? Why so random?

And then like a cold

(*dead*)

finger tracing the length of my spine:

Christopher died March 16th—3/16.

Mike died September 14th—9/14.

"I want to wake up, I want to wake up, I want to wake—"

Something in my peripheral vision again. East again. By the road again.

I don't want to look.

You have to.

I turned and looked. The silhouette of a man again. Next to him, the silhouette of a boy. They were holding hands, looking to cross the road and journey into the field beyond together.

I know who they are.

So follow them.

I'm scared.

You? Scared?

Yes.

The man and boy both glanced back towards me, their faces still shrouded in shadows, but I knew who they were.

I know who they are.

The man and boy crossed the road and started into the field.

Go after them. Maybe they have something to show you.

CHAPTER 16

Go after them.

They're not real. I know I'm dreaming.

Go after them, they want to show you something.

I just want to wake up.

I started after them, stunned but not stunned by my pursuit. Fever dreams are like being a part of a puppet where only the head is under your control.

You are helpless to some unseen force that takes you places you would never willingly go, shows things you would never willingly see, and—because of that one sinister exception to the puppet rule, granting you control of the head, and the head only—lets you absorb and digest and relive the anguish you would never willingly court.

.   .   .

And so I went after them. What choice do puppets have?

I had to run to keep up. They were already halfway through the field when I decided to call to them. I did not use their names. I was too afraid to use their names. What if it *was* Mike and Christopher? I didn't want to see them. Not like this. I was afraid to see them like this.

How else would you see them, Maggie?

You know what I mean. It would be bad...the dream would make it bad...

Still I followed without giving my legs permission. I was in the field now, maybe fifteen yards behind them. I called to them again, still refusing to use their names. My shouts were monosyllabic commands and pleas. *"Stop!" "Wait!" "Please!"*

The field dropped suddenly downward, almost as if crumbling away. And maybe it had, only the prison of my mind obeyed the rules of the waking world—the illogical and the bizarre and the fantastically cruel were as uninhibited as they wanted to be.

This time was no different.

The field *had* crumbled away. I now stood at its edge. Below was a graveyard. The man and the boy were there. Though it defined futility, I called to them a final time.

"I know who you are! I know what you're doing!"

Do you?

I dropped my head and shut my eyes tight. "I just want to wake up..."

I opened my eyes and found myself standing in the graveyard. I was alone.

I began to wander. All of the tombstones were blank. Even in the teasing light of the moon, I could see they were all blank.

Except for one.

I was maybe ten feet away, close enough to see that the stone had been engraved, yet too far to make it out.

But you know whose grave it is, don't you?

Yes.

Again my legs betrayed my will and made me approach. The grave was freshly dug, the rectangular hole six feet down into the earth. The tombstone...was not Christopher's?

#bq-ctr I AM NUMBER SIX.

That's what the tombstone read.

"I am number six," I said aloud. What did that mean? An Ebenezer Scrooge kind of thing maybe? Seeing my own tombstone? I'm killing myself with the drug, and Mike and Christopher are like Ghosts of Christmas Future trying to warn me, was that it?

Then wouldn't that make you number three? Christopher is one, Mike is two...

I looked around the graveyard. Now I *wanted* to find Mike and Christopher. To have them appear and explain it all.

"*Hello!?*" I called in all directions.

Say their names.

I closed my eyes and took a long, steadying breath. My tone was soft and hesitant; I couldn't manage anything else.

"Mike...? Christopher...?"

"Mom?"

My eyes popped open. I whirled on the spot. "*Christopher?*"

"Mom?"

It was coming from below. From the grave.

I approached the grave's edge. Christopher was there, looking up at me. He did not look as he had when he died. He was youthful and vibrant looking. He could have been a healthy boy fooling about in a cemetery who happened to tumble into an open grave, now hoping his mother would fish him out of such a scary spot.

I did not crawl or climb but *jumped* into the grave after him. I expected the earth to be solid, the jump to punish my knees and ankles, but the earth was soft. Unnaturally soft. It swallowed my legs up to the knee. I immediately braced my hands on either side of me and went to push myself out, but my hands merely sank into the earth, affording me no leverage. I needed Christopher's help.

Of course he was gone now.

I was alone in the open grave, stuck up to my knees. I began a frantic dig. If I couldn't push myself to the surface, I would have to dig my way out.

I dug furiously around my knees, scooping up handfuls of dirt in both hands and tossing them into the farthest corner of the grave. All I needed was to clear my ankles; from there I felt certain I could pull one foot free, and then from there the other.

Except with each scoop tossed, it seemed as if the divot I'd created would regenerate, produce more soil. The faster I dug and tossed, the quicker the soil would replace itself. I was a woman making a futile attempt at bailing out a boat destined to sink. However, if there was one saving grace, it was that I was *not* sinking—I remained no deeper than up to my knees; the soil around me was not rising.

And then Mike appeared at the base of the grave with a shovel in his hand, eager to change that.

CHAPTER 17

Mike lobbed a shovel of dirt into the grave, hitting me in the face. I wiped and spat it away and then looked up at him in disbelief.

"*What are you doing!?*"

He continued lobbing shovelfuls of soil into the grave as he spoke. His tone was conversational and airy. "You want to die, right? So you can be with Christopher again?" He threw another shovelful at my face and, with a look of contempt, added: "Oh, and me, of course."

I wiped and spat soil away again. "No, no, I was wrong—I don't want to die."

Mike continued shoveling, his contempt for me gone, the airy tone back. "Too late."

"Mike, no! I'm sorry! *Please stop!*"

He did. But not because I'd asked him to. He stopped because someone had now joined him at his side. My oldest brother, Dave.

"Take a break, Mike," Dave said.

Mike smiled, handed Dave the shovel, and patted him on the back. Over his shoulder as he went to leave, he said: "See you soon, Maggie."

"*Mike, wait! Oh God, MIKE!!!*"

"Would you shut up already?" Dave said to me. "You always were such a baby." He scooped up a big shovelful of soil and grinned.

Through fog and night, his grin somehow shone down on me, illuminating the malevolence in his intent. "Now we're gonna have some fun. You remember this, don't you? No quilt and closet to wrap you up and stuff you in, but this is just as good—*better* even."

My pulse hammered in my chest like war drums. "*Dave, please!!!*"

He laughed as he lobbed shovel after shovel of soil.

"*Please!!!*"

Shovel after shovel, now chanting his trademark mantra from our childhood: "*Smother! Smother! Smother! Maggie cries just like her mother!*"

"*PLEASE!!!*"

He stopped. Stabbed the shovel into the earth and began rubbing his right palm. There was a sizable wound on it. He winced as he rubbed. "Where do you suppose this came from?" he asked me. He started wandering away, all of his attention now on his wounded palm, as though I had never been there.

The soil was up to my waist now. I fought and wriggled, but it was futile.

"*Help me! Someone, help me!!!*"

A third visitor appeared at the base of the grave. A man. His face, his body, inexplicably cloaked in shadows no matter which direction he moved. A phantom.

"Please, help me," I called up to him.

He grabbed the shovel, scooped up a mound of soil, and looked down at me with a face that held no features, only darkness.

"Scared?" he asked.

"Yes," I said desperately, all pride gone.

"Good. Then look over there, please."

I followed his gaze to the left of the grave where a video camera on a tripod stood tall, its little red eye glowing, recording, the camera lens angled downward, pointing directly at me.

"You are number six," he said to me and began lobbing soil into my grave, keen on burying me alive.

. . .

I knocked on the door of room 12. Morris answered. My appearance woke him faster than caffeine ever could.

"Jesus, Mags, what is it?"

In retrospect, I feel a little embarrassed by it, but at the time, all I could do was hug him and start crying.

. . .

Sitting on Morris's bed, the crying over, my account of the dream told, I turned to him and said: "Our guy...it's about fear...it's *all* about fear."

CHAPTER 18

Dr. Cole opened his notebook and clicked a pen. "Whenever you're ready, Maggie."

"It's not Irony Appreciation Day today, Dr. Cole," I said.

"No?"

"Nope. It's Martyr Day."

Dr. Cole gave the same accommodating little smile he always gives when I try for levity when dealing with something heavy.

"Suffering for your cause?" he said. "I imagine every day for you since our last session has been Martyr Day."

"Well, then today is Super Duper Martyr Day."

His accommodating little smile became genuine, adding a tiny crinkle around his eyes. "Tell me," he said.

"I drank too much the other night," I said.

"You drank too much while taking a full dose of the drug."

"Yes."

Dr. Cole was the only person (well, besides Morris now) who knew about the bad dreams that came as a result of too much alcohol on the drug.

"Why?" he asked.

"Mike's death hit me very suddenly."

"*Mike's* death?"

I nodded at him knowingly. "Yeah. I guess it finally hit me. Maybe not a knockout punch or anything, but enough to make me order a third glass of wine."

"How much did you end up drinking?"

"Just the three glasses."

Dr. Cole frowned a bit. "Well, that doesn't seem too excessive."

"I didn't think so either. I guess you never can tell with a drug like this, can you?"

Dr. Cole didn't answer, just scribbled some notes. He then asked: "Any sickness the following day? Feverlike symptoms like the time before?"

"No. Perhaps the extra glass of wine combined with the drug was enough to trigger the dream, but not enough to make me sick."

Again, Dr. Cole didn't reply, only scribbled more notes.

"Tell me about the dream," he said.

.　　.　　.

When I'd finished telling him, and when he'd finished taking it all down, he set his notebook and pen aside and settled into his chair.

Analysis time.

"Why do you suppose it was Morris who first knocked on your motel room door? Why not Mike or Christopher or your brother David?"

I'd done some analyzing of my own before my session with Dr. Cole. How could I not? I gave him my theory.

"Without Morris, I wouldn't be here, discussing it all with you," I began. "He's the reason I was in that hotel to begin with. He's the reason I chose to go back on a full dose of the drug. His knocking on my door, getting the whole dream started...I guess it's akin to his asking me for help. How's that?"

Dr. Cole gave a small nod. "I'd say that's a solid assessment."

"Do I pass?"

"I'd say we've only just begun."

I sang the chorus to The Carpenters' "We've Only Just Begun."

No accommodating smile at my levity this time. There's a line.

"Sorry," I said.

He ignored my apology and went on. "Your husband and son led you to the open grave. Why do you suppose it was they who led you?"

"At first I thought it was symbolic—like if I kept going on this path with the drug, I would be joining them soon. I thought this especially true when Mike started to bury me, telling me it was what I wanted."

"But you don't think that now?"

"No," I said. "I think that was just my guilt seeping into the dream. My guilt for not mourning Mike's death the way I should be."

"So then what do you think? Why *did* Mike and Christopher lead you to the grave?"

Unlike the Morris-knocking-on-my-door theory, I was less confident with this one. "I don't really know. My gut—my *heart*—wants me to think they were trying to help me. Sounds crazy, right? I mean, it's my dream, after all; the content, no matter how cryptic, is coming from inside *my* head."

"You said the grave read 'I am number six.' What do you think that meant?"

This one was easy.

"Victim number six. The one we found in the open grave in upstate Pennsylvania. That's what it meant."

"And then after that?" Dr. Cole asked.

"*After that?*"

"Recount it for me again, except add your interpretation of *why* it happened, what it meant."

"An essay question?"

Got the accommodating smile this time. Felt like extra credit after the red ink slashes that was my Carpenters bomb.

"Okay," I said. "I jumped into the grave when I thought Christopher was in there. When I sank up to my knees, unable to pull myself out, it was my mind's way of telling me I was trapped. This became all the more evident when my brother Dave appeared and started burying me alive, looking to suffocate me like he did when we were kids."

"Your claustrophobia."

"Yes."

"His chant about making you cry like your mother."

I frowned. "Well, I don't think *that* really meant anything. It was just something he always used to say—I probably dreamt it to give the whole thing more authenticity, make it all the more frightening."

"You don't see your mother's frequent tears at the hands of your father, and then later your older brothers, as relevant?"

"No."

"You often consoled your mother after her torment; and she, you. What was it you did for her?"

"I just hugged her, that's all."

"And what did she do for you?"

"She sang to me."

"What did she sing?"

"'All the Pretty Little Horses.' All due respect, Dr. Cole, I think we're getting off track."

He did not look as if he agreed, but he nodded anyway, gesturing for me to continue.

.   .   .

"When Dave was burying me, he suddenly complained of a wound on his right palm," I said. "This told me there was a strong connection between our guy and what Dave was doing."

"The wounds on the right palms of all the victims."

"Yup. When the faceless man appeared after Dave and asked me if I was scared, and I admitted I was, he said he was glad and asked me to look at the camera fixed by the grave."

"You already stated you believe your guy is using photographs or video of his victims as his trophies."

"Yes."

"And you believe victim number six had a fear of being buried alive, not unlike your claustrophobia."

"Yes."

"And you now believe your guy's primary fantasy is all about fear; it's what he aims to capture on film."

"I'm pretty confident. But it's *true* fear he's after. Fear of death is not enough for this guy. The burning of the homeless man after he'd somehow revealed his horrific fear of fire makes all the more sense now. In light of my theory, our SAC gave us the green light—grudgingly, I think, but we're desperate—to dig deeper into the victims' pasts. To see whether they *did* have significant phobias and, if so, to see if they sought help for them. See whether there's a connection somewhere."

"And what about the excessive bludgeoning?" Dr. Cole asked. "What ultimately kills them."

"I don't know that yet," I said.

"The wounds on the right palm?"

"I don't know."

"But you feel strongly that his primary urge, what fuels his fantasy, is all about exploiting men's fears."

"Yes."

"Why would a man feel the need to do such a thing to other men, do you think?"

I shrugged. "Lots of reasons. He has his own deep-seated fears, maybe. Those fears make him feel like less of a man. Seeing other men freak out might eradicate those insecurities."

"Have you considered the possibility that he was heavily bullied as a child? That perhaps his victims are all culprits?"

"A bullied kid exacting revenge years later?"

"Yes."

"It's a good theory. Morris originally considered it before I came on board, but the significant discrepancy in age of all the victims—nineteen to sixty-five—makes the theory highly unlikely. Still, Morris dug; who said the bullies had to be our guy's peers, right? Adults can be just as cruel to children."

"Sad but true."

"Yeah, well, background checks have the victims' places of birth spread out all over the East Coast. Morris even dug a little deeper in the lottery-winning chance all victims might have relocated to the same town at one point or another. No luck."

Dr. Cole picked up his notebook and pen again. "So, in conclusion…"

"What do we have, you mean?"

"Yes," he said.

I took a deep breath. "What we likely have is a guy who abducts men of all ages and races, finds and exploits their darkest fears, and then somehow, for reasons we don't know, wounds their right palms, and then gratuitously bashes their heads in, all while filming it."

I considered my spiel. Out loud it didn't sound like much at all. In fact: "I walked in here this morning thinking we'd had a breakthrough. Now I'm not so sure. It still seems too conjecturish."

"Why not wait until you and Morris do your investigating this afternoon—perhaps you'll look back at this fear theory of yours as the most significant catalyst in solving the case."

"I'd like to be there now, looking back on it all."

"I'm sure."

With a tiny smirk, I said: "You know, Dr. Cole, if you're right, if this fear theory I got from my dream *is* the primary catalyst in solving the case, then I have drugs and alcohol to thank for it."

Dr. Cole shook his head, the accommodating little smile there, but only just.

I decided to quit while I was ahead. "Same time next week?"

CHAPTER 19

We knew about Hal's fear of fire. Victim number six in upstate PA had yet to be identified, so no verification on fear of being buried alive was forthcoming anytime soon. So we decided to continue moving backwards from most recent. That left us with victim number five: Douglas Caley, the nineteen-year-old in southeastern Pennsylvania, a junior at West Chester University. All the hallmarks of our guy were there: the cuffs, the excessive head trauma, the lesions on the right palm.

Now we were hoping to test my theory.

.   .   .

"So have you given any thought to what this one's phobia might be?" Morris asked on the drive to West Chester.

"Assuming my theory is correct."

"You seemed pretty damn certain the other night at the motel."

"If you'd had the dream I had, you'd feel pretty certain too."

"That drug, man. If your theory *is* correct, we can add psychic dreams to its list of side effects."

"As long as you mix it with alcohol. And I had no premonitions; all the evidence was there. My dream just organized it a bit."

Morris grunted. "Anyway…Thoughts on this one's phobia then?"

"I have no idea. How can I? It could be fear of clowns for all I know."

"Lots of people are afraid of clowns. You might be right."

I didn't say anything.

"We should be going to the crime scene in Coatesville so you can do your Carnac stuff there," Morris said, "not where the kid went to school."

The student's body had been discovered in the trunk of his own car in Coatesville, Pennsylvania, about twenty miles west of West Chester University. The body was only discovered after neighborhood kids playing nearby complained of the smell.

"The crime scene is probably only a dumping spot," I said. "Besides, Coatesville PD was thorough—they didn't get anything."

"Yeah, I read the file—doesn't mean *you* wouldn't get something. That's the whole point of this experiment, isn't it? Local PD got nothing at the makeshift grave in upstate PA, and then you come along, and suddenly we've got a microfiber cloth that snowballed into the very strong possibility that our guy's trophies are film or video."

"We got lucky with the grave in upstate PA because our guy was interrupted doing his thing. That won't be the case with the prior five. Our guy's too careful to just leave their bodies when he's finished with them."

"He left the homeless guy."

"After setting him on fire in the hope that there'd be nothing left by the time he was found."

"If he hadn't been interrupted in upstate PA, our guy would have probably buried number six on the spot," he said.

"Right—" I said, feeling as though Morris had no heart in his own debate, but was just using (and annoying) me so he could think aloud. "*Buried* him. Who knows when he'd have been found, if ever."

"So you think digging around the university is the way to go."

"I think questioning students and professors is a good start, yes."

"Local PD already did that. No leads."

"Maybe they didn't ask the right questions."

"Like what? What was he afraid of?"

"Yes," I said straight-faced, despite Morris's hint of sarcasm.

Morris went quiet for a minute. Then: "You know, even if we do manage to find out about some kind of phobia with this victim, or *any* of the victims, what does it really give us?"

I frowned, confused. "What do you mean?"

"I mean what I said. What does it give us?"

"Our guy has to find out about these victims' phobias some-how, right?" I said. "I'd say finding his method would be a damn good lead, wouldn't you?"

"He only needed to ask the homeless guy."

"After drugging him. And we've already agreed that Hal was an exception to his type—a one-night stand. Much as it kills me to say, the bastard got lucky Hal was as terrified of fire as he was. We need to focus on the other six if we want to see his typical methodology at work."

.   .   .

Morris went quiet for another minute. Then: "You ever figure out the cuffs with Hal? Why our guy didn't put them on his victim when he had him unconscious? He shackled him, but no cuffs."

"Honestly? I think cuffing Hal was part of the fantasy for that particular one. Our guy had to improvise with Hal to make it worthwhile."

"So cuffing all the others was to immobilize, but for Hal it was to…?"

"It was *ultimately* to immobilize, but there was more to it than that. I think our guy—ugh, and I'm going to use one of your per-verted metaphors again—was doing everything possible to get his rocks off with such short notice. Like I said, his finding out about Hal's fear of fire was a bonus, but it still wasn't enough; he needed more. So I think he wanted to scare a man with no life-leverage so intently, he could make him his slave. It was a total power trip."

"So he's taking chances, growing bolder," Morris said.

"Maybe," I said. "Or maybe just for that one. Remember, Hal was atypical."

"So, going back to the other six victims, finding our guy's method of discovering their phobias…"

"Yeah?"

"You think he'd be dumb enough to use the same method each time?"

"We can hope."

Morris grumbled under his breath.

"What?"

"*Everyone* has phobias, Mags. Yours is claustrophobia. Mine's my ex-wife. There are *millions* of ways he could have found out."

"Any old phobia won't do," I said. "It has to be extreme. Our guy *chooses* these victims, Tim. He researches them like a project. There had to be something special about this college kid—that's why our guy chose him."

"So, find the phobia, and then, more importantly, find out who knew about it and how."

"More or less."

Morris grumbled again.

CHAPTER 20

Joe Pierce sat at his desk, eyes on his PC monitor, yet his mind far away.

"Yo, Pierce."

Startled back to life, Joe looked up and found Paul Jennings leaning over the edge of one of his cubicle walls. Paul Jennings was popular among the men and women in his office. He'd spoken to Joe a few times, but never by name. Always "man" or "buddy" or "pal" or "slick."

Today it was Pierce. He couldn't believe it. Cool guys always called each other by their last names.

"What's up, Jennings?" Joe said. He did not smile. It would be pussy to smile.

Jennings leaned further over the cubicle wall, spoke in just above a whisper.

"Bennett, Miller, and me are going to hit up McCalley's for a few necessary libations. You in?"

It was out of Joe's mouth before he could stop it. "But it's lunchtime," he said.

"Yeah? So?"

Joe began to stammer. He bit his inner cheek to fight it, but the stammer had the insistence of hiccups. "No, no, I, uh...I was just..."

Jennings leaned away from the cubicle and raised his hands. "It's cool, man. Forget it."

He was back to "man" again.

Joe quickly shifted in his chair, leaned in with an eager whisper, hoping Jennings would lean back in as he just had, begin whispering again too: two cool guys planning something bad.

"No, no, it's cool, Jennings. I was, I was, I was—" *Stop stammering!!!* "I was just—"

Jennings raised his hands again. "It's all good, pal. Catch you later."

Pal...

Jennings turned and walked a few feet to where Bennett and Miller were waiting. They formed a small huddle as Jennings whispered something to them. Bennett shook his head and made a face. Miller said something, and they all chuckled softly.

Joe didn't have to hear them to know what they'd said.

Pussy.

Faggot.

You know his real name is Jody, *don't you?*

That's a girl's *name!*

Perfect fit!

And then the laughter.

All three of them left the office. Joe sat in his cubicle feeling sick. He was not aware that his right fist was clenched so tightly that his fingernails were biting into his palm.

A female co-worker who'd witnessed the incident wheeled her chair from her cubicle to Joe's. He did not notice her arrival until she placed her hand on his clenched fist and said: "I'll have lunch with you, Joe."

Joe looked at his co-worker as if he meant to kill her then and there.

Through clenched teeth, he quietly hissed, "*I do NOT need your help,*" and ripped his fist out of her grasp.

Stunned, the co-worker wheeled herself back to her own cubicle without another word.

*   *   *

Still at his desk, rage pulsing, Joe Pierce eventually opened his fist and studied it. His fingernails had cut deep into his palm, slicing open the scar tissue that had been there for decades.

CHAPTER 21

The associate vice president for student affairs and dean of students at West Chester University was exceptionally thorough in organizing everything we needed beforehand. Students and professors were literally seated in a row outside the dean's office, waiting to be interviewed by us as though they were all applying for the same job.

Morris and I didn't waste time asking all the rudimentary questions about Douglas Caley—strange behavior, enemies, etc. Local PD had already done a solid investigation and given us anything we could use, which, unfortunately, was little.

So we got right down to it.

.   .   .

"Were you aware of any phobias the victim might have had? Nothing casual. We're talking *debilitating* phobias."

We got plenty of curious eyebrows, but no affirmative nods.

Until the last one (of course).

The victim's roommate during his sophomore year. Andy Wells. Typical college kid whose priorities were in a bong, a bottle, or his pants.

"Terrified of dogs," Andy Wells said. "I mean *terrified*."

"Why do you say it like that?" Morris asked.

"We lived across the street from these five girls, and they were all cute, but there was this one—Carla Bent—that every guy in our house wanted. I mean, she was smokin' hot. We all tried, but you know, she wasn't interested in any of us." He shrugged and made a face as if to say, *win some; lose some.*

I took a stab as to where this was going. "Except for Douglas."

The kid gave a startled frown, as though I'd read his mind. "Right," he said, still frowning curiously. "She liked Doug."

"So what was the problem?" Morris asked.

"Nothing at first. They dated, and the lucky guy got to hit that—uh...he got to date her for a while."

I often forgot how chock-full of primates college was. "What happened?" I asked. "Why did they split?"

"Carla bought a dog," he said. "One of those stupid little toy things you see celebrities carrying around in their purse."

"Doug was afraid of it?" Morris asked.

Andy Wells gave an incredulous snort. "Yup. I'll never understand it. I mean, *Carla Bent*?" He snorted again. "She could have bought a fifty-foot alligator as a pet, and I wouldn't have cared."

"So what happened?" I asked.

"Doug broke up with her. Didn't give a reason or anything, just something like it wasn't working out or whatever."

"How'd you get the truth out?" Morris asked. "I imagine being afraid of a tiny little dog wasn't something he willingly shared."

"We were all wasted one night. Doug was hammered, and I mean *hammered*. So we're all talking, and we wanted to know why on Earth he would dump someone like Carla. Looking back now, I guess he could have said anything, but like I said, he was wasted. So he told us the truth. Apparently, he was attacked by a dog as a kid and it scarred him for life."

"So what happened after that?" I asked Andy.

"He didn't remember telling us the next day. One of our roommates—John Turner—happily reminded Doug though. Happily reminded *everyone*. John had a serious thing for Carla."

"How did Doug take the news?" Morris asked.

"He kinda closed himself off after that. Stopped hanging with us. Eventually moved out."

"He was your roommate," I said. "Didn't you try to talk to him?"

"We were friends, but we weren't *that* close. I tried talking to him a couple of times, but he just said he didn't want to talk about it, so…you know…" He splayed his hands as if to suggest he'd done all he could've at the time.

"He never suggested he was going to try to get help for his phobia?" Morris asked.

"Not to me," Andy said. His curious frown suddenly came back. "Does this have anything to do with him being killed?"

Morris just said: "Thanks for your time."

CHAPTER 22

Morris and I remained in the dean's office after the interviews. We volleyed thoughts.

"Pretty extreme phobia if you ask me," I said.

"Forsaking the hot girl on campus because of a little doggy? I'd say you're right."

"We should call the boy's home to confirm the dog attack story with his parents. There might be more to it."

Morris nodded in agreement.

"Can I see the file again?" I asked.

He handed it to me.

I eventually found what I was looking for in the autopsy report. "Here," I said. "They found both dog hair and saliva on the victim. Three different breeds. No bites." I looked up from the file.

"I know," he said. "I got excited at first too when the kid said dogs. But Mags, that could have come from anywhere. Strays after he was dumped probably."

"He was dumped in the trunk of a car. Were the strays in there with him?"

"Could have been when he was being dragged to the trunk after he was dead. Or maybe it was already in the trunk. Dog fur is like glue. I guarantee you I've got a pair of pants in my closet some-where with my sister's dog's hair on them."

"Hair *and* saliva? And from three different breeds?" I said.

Morris processed this. Then: "Why no bites?" he asked. "If he really wanted to scare him, why no bites?"

"No idea. Maybe having them crowd him and lick him was enough. You ever been around an excited dog? They can get pretty unruly."

"Or maybe if he got dogs that would bite, our guy would have been worried they'd kill the victim before *he* got the chance."

"Maybe."

"All right, so what's the next move, hotshot?"

"Excuse me?"

"Well, I stand by my previous statement that everyone has at least some type of phobia, but what are the odds that our victim here just happened to have one so debilitating? Your fear theory is looking more and more solid."

"I agree. But why are you asking me about the next move? I'm the consultant."

"With superhero powers and psychic dreams. Maybe we hit up another bar? You could have whiskey with the drug instead of wine this time. Maybe the stronger booze will make it work better."

I felt like punching him. "That's not funny, Tim. Those dreams hurt."

Morris held up a hand, acknowledging that he'd crossed the line. "I'm sorry, Mags. Me asking you the next move is just my way of saying you've been invaluable thus far. I'd still be pulling my hair out over this if you hadn't agreed to help."

I looked at his notoriously depleting hairline. "Looks like I came just in time."

He chuckled and nodded with an expression that said, *I walked into that one...and deserved it.*

.   .   .

"So..." Morris eventually said. "We can confirm victim seven and victim five had extreme phobias."

"Victim seven won't help with our guy's methodology for choosing," I said.

"So, until we get an ID on victim six in upstate PA and are able to start confirming some sort of being-buried-alive kind of phobia, then we only have victim five here," he said. "Maybe I take back what I said about your theory looking more and more solid."

"And your comment about the odds of our victim here having such a debilitating phobia?"

Morris pursed his lips for a moment. "Those *are* pretty slim odds. Tyson/Douglas odds."

"And Douglas won," I said.

Morris looked truly impressed. "*Whoa.*"

"Three brooding brothers and a father who settled all arguments with his fists? I wager I could school you in boxing history. And football. And beer."

Morris held up a hand. "I get it. So do we move on to victim four?"

"I'd like to know if Douglas Caley sought treatment for his phobia," I said. "Maybe local PD can help us with that."

"He might have done it online," Morris said. "Everything's online today. And if he was as ashamed of his phobia as it sounded, he would likely seek anonymity."

"Anonymity online is good for taking the first steps about admitting and sharing and whatnot," I said, "but if he wanted actual help—actual treatment—it would have to be hands-on."

"Our guy wouldn't care about all that. He just wants to find them, find their phobias. He can do that online."

"Then how does he find them; I mean, *really* find them? If the kid wants anonymity, he's not going to offer up anything personal like where he lives and such."

Morris nodded slowly, processing things.

"Maybe our guy wins his trust somehow," I added. "Offers to meet up for a cup of coffee or something someday, swap phobias."

Morris groaned. "You suggesting digging through the internet?"

"Amy Crane—tech analyst in the Baltimore field office. She could do it in a day, with her toes."

"Yeah, I know Amy."

"In the meantime, we can have West Chester PD check out local support groups," I said. "Have them show Douglas's picture around and see whether he attended any."

"You think our guy would go as far as to sit in on meetings up and down the East Coast in order to find victims?"

"You don't?"

Morris sighed. "Yeah…" He looked out the window of the dean's office, the students walking by. "In the meantime?"

"Victim four?"

He looked back at me. "The black guy from Maryland?"

"We can have Baltimore start the ball rolling until we get there. We can give them the particulars when we call Amy Crane," I said.

"They're not gonna go for it, Mags. It's a theory—an agent on bereavement's theory."

"So we tell them what we just found."

"We definitely found something, but it's still early days, Mags."

Now I sighed. "So then you tell me; what should we do in the meantime? Hang around campus? Hit up a frat party?"

"Oh, they'd like you. Spirited little redhead who knows about boxing and beer?"

"I'm serious, Tim. We can't just stay in West Chester."

"Actually, we can," he said, his face and tone becoming professional again. "If we get any hits from local PD about support groups in the—"

I interrupted him. "They're not going to be getting anything anytime soon—"

He held up a hand, telling me to let him finish. "If we get any hits from local PD about support groups in the area, great. If not, Amy Crane might very well have something for us before the day's out. I don't feel like driving all the way to Maryland and back in twenty-four hours, do you?"

"That's the job," I said.

"Maximum efficiency is the job."

He was right. Journeying all the way from Pennsylvania to Maryland only to get a hit about something here, making us have to turn around and journey all the way back, would not be the most efficient use of time.

"Okay, fine; we stay here," I said. "And do what?"

"I could use a bite. We'll bring victim four's file with us and pore over it during lunch."

"I read victim four's file," I said. "I didn't find anything."

"And that's why we're going to read it again."

I pursed my lips. "Fine. You're buying lunch."

"I fly, you buy—you know the rules."

"I'm not *allowed* to fly. I'm a flight risk. I might have one of my Carnac moments and run us off the road. Sorry, exception to the rule this time: You're flying *and* buying."

CHAPTER 23

Victim four was a black man from Baltimore, Maryland, thirty-four, married with two kids, and found just like all the others: cuffed, bludgeoned excessively, lesions on the right palm. I'd been over the file a few times already, hoping something I'd missed would jump out at me, but so far I had nothing. My grumbling stomach wasn't helping.

"I think they went to China for our food," I said. We'd stopped at a little Chinese restaurant on the outskirts of West Chester, hoping for any or all of the following three things to occur while we ate:

1. Amy Crane, the tech analyst from the Baltimore field office, calling with something useful about West Chester University student Douglas Caley's use of the internet when it came to treating his extreme phobia of dogs. Chat rooms, private forums, that kind of thing.

2. Local PD getting a hit after canvassing surrounding phobia support groups in the area with Douglas Caley's photo to see whether he might have attended any, perhaps under a pseudonym.

3. Our guy walking into the Chinese restaurant and confessing to every damn thing while we waited (forever) for our food to arrive.

.   .   .

"I heard it's different over there," Morris said.

"What is?" I asked.

"The Chinese food in China—I heard it's different. This is like *American* Chinese food. Apparently they don't use as many sauces over there as they do over here. It's an American thing—sauce on everything."

I sipped my tea. "I wish I had the last twenty seconds of my life back."

Morris smiled. "Anything popping out at you from the file?"

"No."

"You think it's strange he hunted outside of his own ethnicity?"

"Assuming he's a white male?" I said.

"They're all white males."

"Not true. You want me to start rattling off names?"

"I'm speaking in percentages, and you know it."

"Fine. Assuming our guy is a white male, then no, I don't think it's strange he's hunting outside of his own ethnicity. If our guy's primary fantasy really is all about exploiting phobias in men, then race or size or age is irrelevant. The phobia is all that matters."

"Why no women with phobias?" he asked.

"My guess? It's a macho kind of thing. Our guy gets a high off seeing men squirm. In his eyes, it's okay for women to be afraid of things. But men? Men should be fearless."

"You've been giving this some thought," he said.

"Dr. Cole helps me organize my mental file."

"I see." Morris sipped his tea. "Does Dr. Cole have any decent theories?"

"Bullied as a child," I said. "Seeking revenge on his tormenters years later. I told him you'd originally considered it but dug and came up with nothing."

"So what else?" he asked.

I shook my head. "That was his only theory."

"No, I mean you. Any more insight? You seem pretty sold on the machismo angle."

"It's too early yet."

"I'm not asking you to sign anything. I'm just spitballing here until our food arrives."

"*If* it arrives." I glared in the direction of the kitchen.

"Just spitballing," he said again.

"I've only got a lump of clay right now, Tim. Was our guy bullied growing up? Is he a milquetoast husband who feels emasculated by his domineering wife for 'not being a man'? Is he a ridiculously violent alpha male who loathes weakness? All of these possibilities carry a similar theme, but they're still just a lump of clay." I sighed. "Better than a mountain of clay, I suppose."

"I was sitting on that mountain before you agreed to help," he said.

"You flatter me."

"Maybe soon you'll be telling me your lump of clay has taken shape."

I shrugged. "Maybe."

Our food arrived. I said nothing about the wait.

When the waiter left, Morris said: "You were polite, given all the fuss you made."

"I might want dessert," I said. "I don't want them to spit in it."

.   .   .

The Hunger Gods were in good spirits, waiting until Morris and I were done with our meal before summoning Amy Crane to contact us.

"Amy, hi," Morris said, setting his teacup aside and wiping his mouth with the back of his hand. "What do you got?"

I blindly fiddled with a sugar packet as they spoke.

"Uh huh," Morris said. "Uh huh…yeah…okay…" Both eyebrows suddenly jumped. "*Really*? Are you sure?" He then started nodding apologetically, as if she could see him. "No, no, I know—I'm sorry…" He started fumbling in his breast pocket for his pen and notebook. "Can I have it?"

Morris scribbled something down. I tried to read it, but my inverted vantage point coupled with Morris's chicken scratch meant I'd have to wait.

He eventually hung up. "Touchy, touchy," he said.

"You second-guessed her."

"I didn't. I was just excited, is all."

I waved an impatient hand at him. "What'd she give you?"

"Two online support groups for extreme phobias from the same IP address. *Douglas Caley's* former IP address. Seems he didn't try too hard for anonymity: DC was the screen name he used for both online forums. Both forums had a private message option. Amy was able to gain access, of course."

"Of course."

"One forum was a bust. But the other showed an exchange of messages between a DC and a K4JJ6. The two struck up an online friendship."

"Trace on the IP address for K4JJ6?" I said.

"Multiples, unfortunately. From as far as Boston, to the university library here."

"*Here?*"

Morris nodded. "Unfortunately, security cameras in the library were down during the time period of the email exchange. No luck there."

"So that means our guy had already located Douglas, yet still continued to message him from what was basically Douglas's backyard," I said.

Morris nodded again. "Still gaining his trust, I'd guess. If Douglas Caley ultimately balked at the idea of meeting up, our guy could have gotten him the hard way and ambushed him."

"But he didn't have to, did he?" I said. "That's what Amy gave you."

He touched the tip of his nose. "Bingo. DC and K4JJ6 *did* agree to meet up for coffee in town."

"How far?"

"I could literally throw a stone."

"So we're heading there now," I said.

"We are."

I opened the file, found a recent photo of Douglas Caley, and placed it on top. "Amy give you anything else?" I asked.

"She's emailing the extent of their exchange online. She said it's pretty bland, nothing good. I'd like to be the judge of that, but I don't dare tell her."

"Good idea."

Morris pushed back his seat and stood. "You ready to go see if anyone at that coffeehouse remembers K4JJ6?"

CHAPTER 24

The majority of employees at the Cuppa Fix coffeehouse knew who Douglas Caley was, but not at first sight.

They'd initially furrowed their eyebrows at Douglas's photo, yet when they were told his name, eyebrows came undone and eyes went wide with recognition. *He's the guy who was murdered, right?* they'd all but unanimously said.

A college town was not likely to forget anything like that soon. Ghost stories about Douglas Caley were probably already part of the town's lore. Sad part is, when we catch the son of a bitch, everyone will remember *his* name and forget Douglas's. Nobody remembers the victims—only the monsters.

· · ·

One employee in particular remembered Douglas Caley, not for the obvious, but for his unusual order.

"It was a regular latte," Jen Carr, a twenty-something waitress, told us, "but he always wanted it burnt. The milk, I mean. I was the only one who could do it the way he liked it, so he always sought me out to make it for him." She shrugged and said: "I just stuck it in the microwave for a while. Big whoop."

"How often are you here?" Morris asked her.

The three of us stood on the sidewalk, a few doors down from the Cuppa Fix. Jen Carr took the opportunity to spit her gum on the street and pull a pack of cigarettes from her apron and light one. "Every day," she said, exhaling smoke with her words. "Envy me."

"Would you consider Douglas Caley a regular?" Morris asked.

She smirked. "Not anymore."

Morris did not look amused. He stared at her hard and unblinking for several beats before calmly yet authoritatively asking: "If Douglas Caley were to bump into you on the street, would you recognize him?"

I expected her to give some wisecrack about zombies or something, but Morris's icy gaze had snuffed her bravado. I'd seen him do it countless times. The know-it-all hotshot—girl or boy—angry at the world and seemingly intimidated by no one, until Morris all but climbed inside their psyche and let it be known that they were mere minnows in his world of sharks.

"Maybe," she said more politely now. Her cigarette was finished. She stubbed it out on the ground but did not flick the dead butt away as she had her gum. She held it until we were done. "But I gotta be honest; if it wasn't for his insistence on me making his lattes for him, I probably wouldn't remember him. We get pretty slammed in the morning."

"*How* you remember Douglas Caley is irrelevant," Morris said. His gaze and tone were still icy and firm. More so. "Point is, you *do* remember him, correct?"

"Yes."

"Did he usually come in alone?"

"I don't know. I think so."

"Did he usually get his latte to go?"

"Yeah—*no, wait!* He stayed in-house once. I remember because his insistence on a burnt latte ended up cracking the porcelain. I left it in the microwave too long."

"Okay, good," Morris said. "Now, I want you to think very hard and very carefully on this one, Jen: When Douglas Caley decided to take his coffee in the store that day, was he alone?"

"I doubt it," she said quickly. "I mean, he usually got it to go. Why would he choose to sit this time if—"

Morris raised a hand, cutting her off like a switch. "You're jumping to a logical assumption. That's okay; it's natural. What I'm asking you to do is stop and think. Really think. Try to recall that day as best you can. The weather, what you were wearing, what songs might have been playing in the shop that day. No detail is insignificant. Close your eyes if you think it will help."

Jen Carr closed her eyes.

Most people I've met typically scoff at this method of recall. And I would have to agree that on the surface, it seems a little futile. Don't remember? No worries. Try hard and think about the weather. How 'bout now?

But here's the thing: It usually works. And as usual, the devil was in the details.

It's kind of like what Morris just said about jumping to assumptions. Too many people try to jump ahead and recall the finish line without first recalling the journey. Our minds are computers, and whether we're aware of it or not, they usually catch everything. Problem is, our computers are run by morons—us.

The solution? Try to recall all of the little details we have unknowingly recorded along the way to the finish line. If you're lucky, *A* might lead to *B* might lead to *C* might lead to *D* and so on until your prize is waiting for you at the end of that finish line, clear as can be.

At least that's the objective. Some computers are beyond repair. Some are better than others. Since taking a full dose of the drug, I felt like my computer had a cocaine-fueled Stephen Hawking clacking away for me. And that was the point, I guess. Wish I had more control over it, though. It would be nice to be at my own finish line right now so I could kick this sick bastard square in the nuts.

.   .   .

Jen Carr opened her eyes, her expression one of disbelief, not for what she was about to say, but because Morris's seemingly basic method for recall had actually worked.

"It wasn't me," Jen said. "I mean, I made his latte—burnt the way he likes it—but I wasn't serving him. It was Erin. *Erin* was serving him."

"You made Douglas Caley's latte, but Erin served him?" I asked.

She nodded. "We work in rotation when it's busy. A couple of us will stay behind the counter for a few hours while the others waitress. Then we switch. It's easier this way; we aren't constantly bumping into each other getting our own orders. That day it was my turn behind the counter. Erin was waitressing. She came to me with that guy's order—"

"Douglas Caley," Morris said, not for confirmation, but so that Jen showed the boy respect. I was sure of it.

"Right. She came to me with Douglas Caley's order, saying I would know exactly the way he liked it. That's when I left the cup in for too long and cracked the porcelain."

"You said 'a couple of us' stay behind the counter while the 'others' waitress," Morris said. "Does that mean Erin wasn't the only waitress serving that day?"

"Right—that would have been Stacey too."

"But you're sure it was Erin who served Douglas Caley?"

"Positive. She's the one who brought me his order, told me I would know how he liked it. Plus, she's the one who got the big tip from the other guy."

Morris and I exchanged looks.

"Other guy?" I said.

"Yeah." She chuckled with that previous look of disbelief at her newfound recall. "I'd forgotten all about it until you made me remember just now. There was a guy with Douglas Caley. I never saw him, but apparently he tipped Erin fifty bucks for just coffee."

Morris whistled. "Fifty bucks just for coffee?"

"I know, right?" Jen said. "But here's the thing: Erin said the guy got angry with her and took it back."

"Took back the fifty bucks?" Morris said.

Jen nodded.

"Why?" I asked.

"I don't remember. I think he was hitting on her or something. She'd be able to tell you better than me. You want me to get her?"

"Please," Morris said.

CHAPTER 25

Erin MacDonald could have been my twin—if I were still twenty-two, that is.

She was short but not tiny, slim but not skinny, and had strawberry blonde hair with green eyes and a slight dusting of freckles around the cheeks and nose.

Damn good-looking girl.

We interviewed Erin MacDonald on the same spot we'd interviewed Jen Carr. Traffic had started to pick up some by then, both on the sidewalk and on the street, so Morris suggested we duck into the little alley adjacent to the shop where they kept their dumpster and employees ducked out to make phone calls and catch a smoke.

. . .

"What can you tell me about the guy?" Morris asked.

"He was kinda plain looking," Erin said. "I only remember him because of the way he acted."

"Height? Build? Hair and eye color?" Morris asked.

"Dark hair...dark eyes too, I think." She looked at the ground as she dug for more. "Average height, I guess. He wasn't tall, but he wasn't short."

"You said he had dark hair," I said. "Was it long? Short?"

"Short," she said. "He looked like a business kind of guy. Like someone who works in an office, you know?"

"What was his build like?" Morris asked. "Skinny? Chubby? Fit?"

"Kinda average." She then winced, as if apologizing for her ambiguity. "I'm not being much help, am I?"

Morris immediately waved a reassuring hand at her. "No, no, you're fine; you're doing fine. Tell me about the way he acted, about this big tip he left you."

"Well, he ended up taking it back," she said. "He snatched it right out of my hand."

"Yeah, Jen said that. Can you tell us what happened?"

"The one guy went outside first—the guy in the photo, the one who was killed."

Morris did not insist Erin show respect for Douglas Caley by making her say his name, the way he'd insisted for Jen Carr. My guess for that reason was easy: Erin was a polite and respectful girl, and it showed. Jen Carr was a bitch, and it showed. Morris never shied away from teaching manners to the Jen Carrs of the world.

"Okay," he said. "Go on."

"So, yeah, the guy in the photo went outside first, and the other guy stayed behind to pay the tab," she said. "He insisted on handing me my tip personally."

"Fifty dollars," Morris said.

"Yeah. I couldn't believe it."

"Why do you think he tipped you so much?" Morris asked. "You think he was making a pass at you?"

"At first I did, but his body language was all wrong."

"What do you mean?" I asked. "Wrong how?"

"Well, usually when a customer hits on you, they never really take their eyes off you, you know? This guy, he kept looking all over the shop as he handed me the fifty, looking at all the customers, like he was trying to impress them more than he was me. He even *announced* that it was a fifty when he handed it to me. Otherwise I might have tucked it away in my apron and never noticed it until later."

"So you think he was just as interested in impressing the patrons as he was you," I said.

"It seemed that way, especially when he started going on and on after he gave me the tip."

"On and on about what?"

"That he was this daredevil kind of guy. Like an adrenaline junkie, you know?"

"You mean like one of those extreme sports guys?" Morris asked.

"Yeah, I guess. Only he didn't look the part. Like I said, his build was pretty average. You expect those extreme guys to be all ripped and stuff. This guy did *not* look like that."

"Did you tell him that?" I asked.

"No way—I had his fifty-dollar bill in my hand."

I smiled. So did Morris.

"When did he take the money back?" Morris asked.

"Not long after. I couldn't stand there and listen to him forever. It was busy. But he was just going on and on, so I guess I kind of interrupted him and told him I had to get back to work. I was really polite about it and tried to seem apologetic, but..." She shrugged.

"No dice?" I said.

"No dice. Before I could blink, he snatched the money back out of my hand and left."

"Did he say anything?" Morris asked.

"He mumbled something, but I didn't catch it. He looked pissed, though."

Morris gave a sympathetic smile. "Would you be willing to meet with a sketch artist, Erin?"

"If you think it'll help."

"It'll definitely help."

"Okay then."

A big truck drove by, kicking up spirals of litter in its wake. When it was gone, the street hummed with one of those loud quiets, like the palpable vibration after the music stops. Erin took this opportunity to look at us both one at a time and then ask: "This guy, the tip guy...is he the one who killed that student?"

"We don't know," Morris said.

Erin folded her arms across her chest and squeezed, as though trying to comfort herself. "Should I be worried?"

Morris assured her she was safe.

I wondered whether our guy—assuming this *was* our guy—hadn't planned on killing Douglas Caley that day but, after the incident at the coffee shop, had become so enraged he could no longer wait; he needed to act sooner than later to appease the rage that was coursing through him. If this were true, it would mean all of his premeditative work could be undone if the right buttons were pushed.

Such a possibility held potential.

CHAPTER 26

Joe Pierce sat in his car in the mall parking lot, his grip on the wheel so tight his knuckles glowed white.

He'd always prided himself on his control; it was what made him impossible to catch. A cool head. No mistakes.

And he was getting better with each one too. Becoming a man. Not a pathetic pussy mama's boy. A man.

The guys at work, the cool guys, they saw it. They'd asked him to hang out. To get drinks at lunch.

Drinks at lunch!

Something only bad boys did. They'd thought he was finally cool enough to include in their adventures. He'd finally earned his shot.

Jennings: "Yo, Pierce…"

Pierce! *Pierce*, they'd called him! How long had he waited!?

"…Bennett, Miller, and me are going to hit up McCalley's for a few necessary libations. You in?"

But then:

Pathetic pussy mama's boy: "But it's lunchtime."

Jennings: "Yeah? So?"

Pathetic pussy mama's boy: "No, no, I, uh…"

Jennings: "It's cool, man, forget it."

Pathetic pussy mama's boy: "No, no, it's cool, Jennings…I was, I was, I was—"

Jennings: "It's all good, pal, catch you later."

Joe Pierce cried out and slammed the bottom of his fist down onto his dashboard. Exited his car and slogged towards the mall entrance with a gait that looked as if he was headed towards the gallows.

．　　　．　　　．

The food court was on the second floor of the mall. It was laughable to think Joe could summon an appetite anytime soon, but he had to try. Skipping lunch would guarantee him a hunger headache later in the day, and the last thing he wanted to tack onto this day was a goddamn headache.

He arrived at the mall staircase and glanced left towards the camera shop he frequented. He saw the shopkeeper, the young stoner-talking guy, elbows on the glass counter as he leaned in towards a pretty young girl, his whole face a confident grin. When the girl smiled back, Joe lost it.

CHAPTER 27

Todd Harper leaned over the glass counter to assist the pretty young girl with her decision.

Also to get a whiff.

The blissful scent of teenage skin, yet to be damaged by life. It was maddening.

Todd pointed his index finger through the glass case. "Can't go wrong with the D3200. I own it myself," he lied.

The girl's eyebrows rose when she settled on the price tag. "It's expensive."

Todd nodded. "It is, yes. I suppose the old saying is true: You get what you pay for." He leaned in closer, smelled again. He all but shuddered. "But I can understand how things might be a little tight for someone your age..." *If there was ever a more fitting double-entendre, I don't know it,* he thought, barely suppressing a grin. "... so here's what I'm willing to do. My boss is out to lunch. What do you say we make that price do a split?" The grin surfaced with a will of its own.

The girl looked confused. "What do you mean?"

Still grinning, Todd said: "What does that price sticker say?"

"Five hundred dollars."

Todd leaned in further still, speaking in a provocative whisper now. "Suppose it reads two-fifty?"

"Can you do that?"

"I can keep a secret if you can." He winked at her.

She smiled back, but it was noncommittal; she was clearly uncomfortable with the situation.

A man entered the store. He did not wait patiently behind the young girl but instead rushed towards her, stomping into place by her side.

Todd Harper recognized him instantly. The weird guy who said he played around in caves.

"*He's a coward!*" the weird guy yelled. He faced the girl, yet his finger was thrusted at Todd. "He told me he was afraid of caves! *He's a coward!*"

The young girl nearly tripped over her own feet in an attempt to back away.

"*Dude!*" Todd said. "What's wrong with you?"

"What's wrong with *me*!? *Nothing's* wrong with me! *You're* the one who's afraid! Something's wrong with *you*!" Turning back towards the frightened girl now: "He's not a real man! He's a coward! *A pathetic pussy coward!*"

The young girl bolted for the exit and disappeared into the crowd that was now gathering.

"Listen, man," Todd warned, "I'm only seconds away from calling the police on your ass."

The man's anger dropped from his face. Mentioning the police had obviously rattled him.

Todd used it. "That's right, pal—*the police!*"

"*Pal?*"

Todd stuck out his chest, relishing the crowd that was accumulating by the second. "That's right, *pal*—" he said again, the word clearly affecting the weird guy as much as mentioning the police had. Maybe more so. "Get your ass out of here!"

The weird man spun and sprinted away, the crowd quickly separating for him as though his lunacy was contagious.

All eyes eventually fell back on Todd. He circled an index finger by the side of his head with animated eyes. "*Cuckoo...*" he sang to the crowd.

He got a few nervous laughs, not the least of them being his own.

CHAPTER 28

We were still in West Chester, Pennsylvania, driving around and waiting to hear whether local PD had gotten any hits on Douglas Caley's photo at any of the support groups in the area that dealt with phobias. And now, thanks to the composite sketch Erin Mac-Donald had just provided, we had another goodie to add to our hopeful hit list.

·　　·　　·

Amy Crane from the Baltimore field office was still doing her thing, but could unearth no more cyber traces between who we hoped was our guy and Douglas Caley, just the initial back and forth between DC and K4JJ6 on the private forum that led to the meeting at the Cuppa Fix that likely, sadly, led to the end for Douglas Caley not long after.

Still, Morris had pored over the transcript of the cyber conversation on the private forum, hoping he might spot something useful despite Amy Crane's insistence there was nothing, and to Morris's disappointment, Amy had been correct. There was nothing.

·　　·　　·

"You've been quiet," Morris said as he made a left and began taking us into a more rural area of West Chester. It was an impressive bit of scenery. Beautiful homes, autumn foliage, clean streets.

"Just thinking," I said.

"Mind sharing?" he asked with not a little sarcasm.

I didn't bite. My mind was still working things out, and I worried that voicing anything would break the rhythm I had going in my head.

"Not right now," I said.

My peripheral vision caught Morris's disapproval. Still, he kept his mouth shut, knowing it was better to let my brain cook a little longer before I served him anything.

"Oh, now we're talking," he said with sudden enthusiasm.

A baseball field came into view as we cleared the hill. It was a Little League game, the boys maybe ten or eleven, stands packed with screaming parents.

"What?" I said. "What're you doing?"

"You keep doing your thing," he said. "I'm grabbing me a hot dog and a seat and enjoying the game."

"Good use of government time," I said.

"Right now all we *have* is time." He pulled into the lot and killed the engine. "Come on, I'll buy you a hot dog."

"We just ate."

He groaned. "Come on, Mags—let's bring back some of those lovely childhood memories of yours. You played baseball to please daddy, didn't you?"

"*Football*," I said as I opened the door and got out.

Morris smiled. "Big shot."

CHAPTER 29

Morris, hot dog in one hand, can of Coke in the other, guided us to a spot at the very top of the bleachers, as far away from the screaming parents as we could get. I'd declined the hot dog and instead settled for an iced tea. Although, now watching Morris cram nearly half of the hot dog into his mouth in one bite, I was beginning to crave one myself.

A hot dog outside at a sporting event was one of the few half-way decent memories I had of my father. He would buy me one, I'd wolf it down to impress him, he'd palm the top of my head and shake it too hard (already on his fourth beer plus whatever he sipped from the flask in his jacket pocket) and ask me whether I wanted another. I'd say yes, even though I didn't, and I'd wolf that one down too. He'd laugh proudly, palm my head too hard, and ask me whether I wanted another. I'd say yes, of course, though my tiny stomach wanted anything but. I would somehow finish that third hot dog below his looming gaze that held an odd mix of both pride for my appetite and a warning if I didn't finish.

Not long after, I would then excuse myself to the bathroom and puke it all up.

This happened three times if I recall correctly. You'd think I'd never want to be within a ten-block radius of a hot dog ever again.

Yet for some reason I craved one now that I was near a ballgame. A bizarre Pavlovian thing if there ever was one, I suppose.

. . .

"Good times," Morris said to me after chasing his mega bite with a swig of Coke. "Brings me back."

"You played baseball?" I asked.

He nodded while taking a second swig from his can. "Catcher. Tough as they came behind the plate."

I rolled my eyes, though I didn't doubt it. I teased Morris as often as possible—hairline; paunch that seemed to gain an inch with each passing year; woefully out of touch with current trends (though the unforgiving hours of the job often made us both guilty of that)—but make no mistake, Morris was as tough as nails.

Still, I had my fun: "You ever play against men, or just boys like these?"

He threw me a look. "I was a boy myself at the time, genius. And yes, I did play against men. High school."

"High school boys are men? That's kind."

"Maybe not up here—" He gestured to his head. "But they sure as hell got the *bodies* of men. Especially nowadays..." He waved a hand over the crowd of parents and the creepily vested interest they had in their children. "Wouldn't be surprised if half these parents are slipping their kids a little something extra along with their Flintstones chewable in the morning."

Morris's words registered deeper than I'm sure he intended. I thought of my middle brother, John. John was the smallest of all three of my brothers. Not so much in height, but in bone structure. He was fine-boned, always getting injured during play. This bothered my father to no end. I can remember waking up one night because I'd heard something in our backyard. I looked out the window and found my father making John do pull-ups on our jungle gym in the dead of night. John had lost a wrestling match earlier that morning.

"You ready to share?" Morris said.

"Huh?" I snapped from my daze, thinking for a brief moment that he was asking me about John.

"You ready to share yet?" he asked again. "You get your thoughts in order?"

I sipped my iced tea and said: "I don't have anything earth-shattering yet. If I was to share, it would insult you."

"Are you fishing?"

"Huh?"

"For compliments?"

I frowned.

"Well, then don't make me tell you how valuable your insight is," he said. "And don't make me go back to *Day 1* stuff about how nothing is insignificant."

I groaned. "Fine," I said. "Our guy's need to exploit men's fears is rooted in some serious insecurities about himself. The big tip for Erin the waitress at the coffee shop; the bragging about how brave he is; how Erin said he seemed more concerned that everyone around him was acknowledging his bravado as opposed to her. Deep down, however, the guy is probably a mess. He desperately wants to feel like a man, or what he perceives to be a man."

"So he's killing men to feel more like a man himself?"

"I don't think the killing part is part of the fantasy. The excessive job he does…it appears to be the only time he loses control. I think when he bashes them, he's bashing himself."

Morris squinted as he processed everything. "So you think by terrifying them first, he reduces these men to reflections of himself."

"Yes."

"So he finds these men, finds their phobias, abducts them, and then torments them with those phobias…"

"Yes."

"At first it is extremely cathartic for him—to watch other men cry and plead. He records it or photographs it so he can revert back to these keepsakes whenever he needs validation for what he perceives to be his own shortcomings…"

"Yes."

"Before long, however, once those keepsakes have been recorded, the squirming, pleading man before him becomes a reflection of himself. It disgusts him, enrages him. So he destroys it. Destroys the part of himself he hates."

"Yes."

Morris let out a long breath, cheeks puffing. He seemed somewhat mollified by his recapping aloud, as though it helped organize his internal hard drive.

·   ·   ·

"What about the right palm?" he eventually asked.

I sighed. "That I have absolutely no clue about."

"You don't want to even try?"

"I wouldn't even know where to begin."

"I'll start then," he said. "The right palms are damaged, but not blatantly. Lab reports say the wounds are not cuts but more like punctures. Surrounding bruises on the palms propose the victims had something pressed into their hands until it damaged the flesh."

"I'm well aware."

"And you don't have *any* theory?"

"I really don't, Tim."

"Well, then *guess*!"

I recoiled as if he'd spat on me.

He immediately hung his head and shook it. "Ah shit...I'm sorry, Mags."

I leaned back in and placed a consoling hand on his shoulder. On the surface was a guy enjoying a hot dog and a Coke at a ballgame, but underneath was a roiling pit of stress. To Morris's great strength of character, this was easily forgotten; he could be affable even when he was moments away from a nervous breakdown.

Morris looked at me with tired eyes and nodded a thanks.

I smiled back at him, but he never saw it; his attention was now towards a sudden commotion in the dugout. A boy was being chastised by his coach, and "chastised" was putting it kindly. The coach looked as if he was ready to belt the kid.

"What's going on?" I asked.

Morris didn't answer, just kept his eyes on the scene below.

I tapped a woman in front of me on the shoulder. She turned.

"What's going on?" I asked her.

The woman shook her head, a sympathetic look on her face. "Coach's son," was all she said.

"What'd he do?" I said.

The woman gave a helpless shrug. "Struck out."

I turned back to the dugout. The boy had since taken his spot on the bench, slumped over, tears threatening, the other boys scooting away from him lest they catch their wrathful coach's eye for daring to acknowledge the boy's existence.

The coach was still purple with rage. He kicked at the fence and cast his son a final, deadly glare. The boy, still slumped, head down, didn't dare meet his father's gaze.

And then things got really bad.

The boy's mother approached the bench to console her son.

The boy—no longer able to fight the actuality that he was indeed still a boy—turned and broke down into his mother's arms.

Coach-slash-father-slash-husband-slash-dickhead stormed over towards his wife and son with such ill intent in his gait it looked as if violence was inevitable.

Morris apparently felt the same way. He took the bleacher benches two at a time as he ran towards the impending scene.

Coach had reached his wife and son. Began shouting abuse at both of them, the mother pulling her son in tight, shielding him from whatever was to come. This only incensed the boy's father further. He reached forward and took hold of his son's arm with both hands, yanking him from his mother's embrace—

—just as Morris reached forward and ripped the father from his son, yanking him backwards, tossing him aside, the father stumbling back and tripping over his own feet, landing smack on his butt.

Embarrassment had the father scrambling back to his feet more than courage did. He did not rush towards Morris as he had his wife and kid, but still approached, and none too pleased.

Morris need only point a threatening finger and state—not shout—a command to stop the man's march cold. He did not even tell the man he was a federal agent, only: "Come one step closer and you're taking a nap."

The father grumbled and cursed and kicked up dirt, but did not dare take a step forward. Morris turned towards the mother and son, but they'd since headed towards the parking lot, likely heading home.

Morris turned back towards the coach whose coloring was just as purple as before, though I'd wager humiliation, not rage, was now the artist for this particular shade. Morris locked eyes with the man until the man was forced to look away, thoroughly defeated.

.   .   .

Morris soon joined me back on the bleachers, all eyes following him along the way.

"Asshole," he muttered as casually as a man disagreeing with something he saw on TV. He picked up his Coke, finished it in a gulp, and then looked at me. "Ready to go?"

CHAPTER 30

It was a strip club that catered to the blue collar. There were more upscale spots in better parts of the city, but those spots weren't for real men. Real men came to spots like this.

Except Joe Pierce didn't feel like a real man today.

He'd grown so much in the past year. Each new victim had been like scratching a fresh line on the wall above the old, measuring his growth as a parent would their child's height.

His confidence often reached peaks he never thought possible. He'd spoken to attractive women without stammering. He'd made eye contact with men. He'd even made a joke in the break room at work that had everyone laughing. Jennings, Bennett, and Miller had been there. They laughed.

He was growing. And fast. The gaps between those lines on the wall becoming further and further apart.

And then Jennings had asked him to join them for drinks at lunch. And he'd blown it. With just one incident—*one!*—all the lines of growth on the wall felt as if they'd been erased.

No. No, he could not accept that. Would *not* accept it.

Oh God, but the scene he'd made at the camera store at the mall…

A real man wouldn't have handled it that way. A real man would have…a real man would have…

Joe grimaced as though in pain. It was all he could do from slamming his fist down onto the bar.

What *would* a man have done? Punched the stoner-talking dude behind the counter? Stood his ground and called the stoner-talking dude's bluff about calling the police? Maybe not even have *been* there to begin with? Kept his cool?

Oh God, how many times had he done this in his lifetime? I shoulda, I shoulda, I shoulda—

This time his fist did pound the bar.

The bartender, a pretty but worn-looking woman, approached. "You okay, sweetie?"

He nodded quickly. "Yeah, I'm okay, uh...I'm okay, uh, sweetie—" *oh Jesus Christ!* "I'm okay...can I have another?"

The bartender turned and went to work on his drink.

One by one, he was losing all he'd gained. Yesterday he wouldn't have stammered when answering the bartender. He wouldn't have been at a loss for a pet name, forced to repeat her own like a damn fool.

One by one...

No.

Goddammit NO.

The bartender brought his drink, a gin and tonic. Joe drained it in two long gulps.

No more tonic next time. Show her you're a man.

"Another," he said as he set the glass down with authority. "Hold the tonic."

The bartender laughed and went to work on his new drink.

She'd laughed. At him or at his joke?

Your joke. Have another drink.

Though he wasn't much of a drinker—it was the one thing he had trouble exorcising from the past—today Joe Pierce was going to change that. He would drink like

(*Dad*)

a man, and he would get a private dance like a man, and he would keep on going until today was but a mere hiccup, and the lines of growth on the wall reappeared one by one…with plenty of room at the top for more.

.   .   .

The bartender brought his drink. He took a big sip and dared wink a thanks at her, the funneling of gin into his virginal liver already giving him nerve.

She smiled back.

No doubt there—that smile was the real deal. He drained his gin and immediately ordered another.

CHAPTER 31

"Superman," I said.

Morris, eyes on the road, frowned as if I'd asked him a riddle. "Huh?"

"You were Superman back there."

He now glanced at me with one eye. "You wouldn't have done the same?"

"Physically? No."

Now he risked taking both eyes off the road. His look said *explain*.

"You think I could have tossed that guy aside the way you did?" I said.

"You'd have hit him."

Very true.

"Probably better you beat me to it then," I said.

He chuckled.

"My heart breaks for that poor kid," I said. "Hope you didn't make things worse for him."

He frowned again, although this frown wasn't trying to solve a riddle: He got it. "Yeah..." he said. Then: "Shit."

"Don't sweat it, Tim. Guy was a bully. Sometimes bullies need a proper dose of humiliation to gain perspective."

"Hope so." His hands were now fists on the wheel.

*　　*　　*

I decided to change course. "So where to now?"

"Don't know. Wait somewhere and hope to hear from local PD about hits on support groups in the area, I guess."

"And if we get nothing?" I asked.

"Hope the John Doe in upstate PA gets a name."

"Why? So we can dig and confirm that he *was* afraid of being buried alive? Big whoop."

"*Big whoop?*"

"I feel like we're doing too much *getting to know you*; not enough *just get you*," I said.

Morris shrugged. "Gotta know your prey before you can hunt it efficiently."

"All we do is hunt. It'd be nice to start trapping."

Morris placed his one eye on me again, a raised eyebrow above it this time. "Why does it feel like we've switched demeanors all of a sudden?"

I leaned the side of my head against the car window, exhaled, and, in a voice that sounded tired even to me, said: "I'm just saying."

"I wouldn't mind if our guy went the way of Dahmer or Heidnik or Bundy," he said.

I lifted my head off the window and looked at him.

"Got careless and allowed one to get away," he elaborated.

I placed my head back on the window. "Our guy's too careful."

He shrugged again. "Until he's not."

CHAPTER 32

Drunk.

No—*wasted.*

How many straight gins had he had? He didn't know. What he did know was that he felt better. He'd watched the dancers doing their thing, and soon built the nerve to tip them when they approached his seat. Most of them would spread their tits and ask him to place the tip between them before pressing them back together, their cleavage swallowing up the cash. He liked that. After his umpteenth gin, he'd insisted on placing the tips in their panties. One of them really liked this request. She'd asked him if he wanted a private dance. He happily obliged.

.　　.　　.

Back behind the curtain in a small room now. They were alone, the stripper nude save for her panties. She gyrated before him and, soon, on him. They didn't do that with just anyone—only real men.

"What's that, sweetie?" she asked.

Had he said something?

"Huh?"

"What did you say?" she asked.

"Real man," he managed.

She smiled and straddled him, grinding herself into his groin. "Yes, you are."

"Yes, I am…" And then: "Say it."

"You're a *real* man," she cooed.

"I'm no pussy mama's boy…"

"No, you're not, sweetie."

He grinned, mumbled: "Not afraid of anything…"

"No, you're not, sweetie."

"No, I'm not, sweetie…" He let out a drunken giggle—he felt just fine about using their pet names back at them now.

She ground harder, pressed her bare breasts into his face. He licked them.

She leaned her torso away and wagged a playful finger at him. "No, no, sweetie," she said.

He frowned. Why not? Didn't she want him to?

"No pussy mama's boy," he slurred again. "Not afraid of anything."

She smiled and turned on his lap, now facing away from him, grinding her ass into his groin. He reached up and around for her breasts. She caught his hands at the wrist and guided them back down.

He reached up and around for her tits again, and again she guided his hands back down.

Why *not*?

She leaned back into him, resting the back of her head into his chest. Looking up at him with a patient smile, she said: "Just the dance, sweetie."

"It's okay…it's okay…I'm not afraid of anything, okay?" he slurred. "Those other guys were, but *I'm* not, okay?"

She took her head off his chest and leaned forward, grinding her ass faster into his groin, hoping to finish him off quickly.

He told her to face him again.

She did. Straddling him once more, patient smile wearing thin, she placed her hands on his shoulders, a strategic placement to block his probing hands at the source.

He cleared both arms away and showed her the palm of his right hand. "You see this? Not anymore...not anymore..."

The patient smile was wary now, the grinding slowing down, concern for her well-being superseding getting him off.

He gripped her ass tight and pulled her back in, picking up her slacking pace with his own determined thrusts upward. "Not anymore." Thrust. "Not anymore." Thrust. "Not anymore." Thrust.

She started pushing against his chest in an effort to free herself.

His grip on her ass tightened. He thrust harder, through gritted teeth said: "See?" Thrust. "*See?*" Thrust. "*Don't need you anymore, bitch.*" Thrust. "*Don't need you anymore, bitch.*" Thrust. "*Don't need you anymore, bitch.*"

She scratched and clawed. "*Let GO of me, freak!*"

Freak!!!???

He grabbed her neck and slammed her to the floor, keen to choke away her audacity against his manhood.

"*THEY were freaks!*" he screamed into her face. "*THEY were freaks! I fucking showed them that THEY were the freaks, not me! Not me, you fucking bitch! NOT ANYMORE! NOT ANYMORE!! NOT ANYMORE!!!*"

A powerful hand snatched the hair on the back of his head and jerked him to his feet. Now a forearm, thick and solid around his neck like a python on its prey.

Joe gargled and flailed, his efforts laughable in the massive bouncer's grip.

The dancer then became Joe Pierce's ironic savior. She rushed forward and attacked Joe as the bouncer held him. The bouncer yelled at her to stop, was eventually forced to toss Joe aside in order to restrain the dancer's fury.

Joe—on the floor, the room spinning from alcohol and adrenaline and rage—remembered the buck knife in his pocket.

CHAPTER 33

We were seated at an outdoor café. Our usual back and forth had been quiet. Morris fiddled with his phone. I watched the people go by.

Morris eventually lifted his head from his phone. "Looks like our guy finally has a moniker."

My daze broke. Surely I'd misheard him. "*What?*"

"No, not like that. The High Striker—that's what they're calling him now."

"The what?"

"High Striker. It's that carnival game where you hit the mark with a big mallet to test your strength. They're calling him that because of the extreme bludgeoning job he does on them."

"That's ridiculous."

"You ever heard one that isn't? What did they call your buddy Thomas Hays?"

"He had dozens," I said.

"The Cypher Slayer was the one that stuck."

I couldn't hide my disgust. "I'll never understand it, these ridiculous names—we're giving these assholes what they want."

"And what's that?"

"Immortality."

"People are fascinated by the macabre. It's unavoidable."

"It's asinine."

For some reason, Morris sought to justify it. "Sometimes it makes things easier with a name—if for nothing else but convenience in discussion."

"Then how about coward or loser or pathetic douchebag ass-hat? Would be nice if we remembered these monsters for what they truly are and not some iconic persona their sick minds are desperately trying to convey to the world."

"I hardly think The High Striker is flattering."

I shook my head. "It's something, though."

Morris conceded my point by sipping his coffee and going back to his phone.

.   .   .

I thought of Dr. Cole, of the pain he went through (and forever *will* go through) after Thomas Hays killed his wife. I thought of how I'd exploited his wife's murder in order to get him to prescribe me more of the drug. It nauseated me. I kept telling myself that I was doing it for a greater good; that by taking the drug and helping Morris, I was pre-empting the Thomas Hayses of the world. I might not be able to get Dr. Cole's wife back, or any of the others back, but I could stop future atrocities, couldn't I? That's why I was here, wasn't it?

And after you catch this one?

I go on to the next.

And after that one?

The next.

You can't catch them all.

I can try.

Until you're dead? Sounds like suicide to me.

It's not suicide.

Let's hope for Mike and Christopher's sake, you're right.

I'm doing a good thing; the right thing.

So it's Super Duper Martyr Day again, is it?

Yes—I'll be forgiven when my time comes.

Oh puh-leeease...

"Mags?"

I blinked. "Huh?"

"You all right?"

I nodded too fast, obvious lie. "Yeah, why?"

"You looked constipated there for a minute."

On this drug? Not a chance.

"I'm fine," I said. "I would just really like to catch this guy."

Morris leaned back in his chair and pursed his lips in thought. "And after that?" he asked.

Christ, was he just in my head?

"I'm not thinking about after that," I lied. "I'm only thinking about this."

Morris nodded slowly, lips pursed in thought again. "In the car, you said you wanted to stop hunting and start trapping."

"That's right. What's the point of knowing our prey if we don't ultimately set a trap for him?" I said.

"Just like that? It's that easy?"

"Let's say we found out everything about this guy, and I mean everything: what his trigger to start killing was, what he does to the right palm of all his victims, his *entire* backstory. So what? We'd still be using that information to hunt him."

Morris's chin retracted as though I was talking gibberish. "*And?* Each new window into our guy's psyche places us a step closer towards why he does what he does."

"But that's just it," I said. "Who *cares* why? Maybe he thinks aliens are making him do it. Maybe he had a Norman Bates kinda thing going on with his mother. Who cares? He's still doing it. We need the how. *How* is he doing it? *How* is he choosing his victims? Not the *why*."

"You say it as though 'how' and 'why' are mutually exclusive. You know better."

I gave a frustrated nod. "I know the two aren't mutually exclusive; of course I know that. I'm just saying…" But I wasn't really sure *what* the hell I was saying.

"Jesus, Mags, we really have swapped demeanors. To think I would be the one telling *you* to be patient."

I exhaled more frustration. "I'm just saying I think we know enough to stop following and start leading."

"Set a trap," he said.

"Yes."

"I'm all ears."

I opened my mouth but had no words. Morris cocked his head and raised both eyebrows at me as if to say, *I'm waiting.*

I closed my mouth, sat back in my chair, and folded my arms across my chest.

"We're still courting the guy, Mags. We'll know when we have enough to propose."

"Please keep your lame metaphors to yourself."

Morris sipped his coffee and calmly looked away, his way of saying, *Young lady, I will not talk to you if you're going to behave like this.*

Thing was, he was right. Of course "why" and "how" aren't mutually exclusive. They're best friends. I just felt like it was all taking too damn long.

But that's okay, right, Maggie? After this guy, there's the next, and the next after that…

Better to catch them sooner than later. It's why I'm on the goddamn drug to begin with.

You were never this impatient before Christopher got sick. You worked all angles. You were meticulous almost to a fault. Why is it different now? Why so impatient?

I don't know.

Could it be that each passing day on a full dose of this crazy drug feels like someone else's hand is on the dial, setting the timer ahead to rob you of your allotted time? A premature heart attack? A nice stroke, maybe?

I don't know what the hell you're talking about.

The will to live is the ultimate lie detector, Maggie. You can't fool it.

It's like I said: Better to catch them sooner than later.

Before what?

Before they kill again, of course.

Is that all?

YES.

Super Duper Martyr Day doesn't have to be a regular holiday, you know. Dr. Cole is right; you do a damn good job without your friend in an Rx bottle.

It's too slow.

You can't catch them all, Maggie.

Morris's cell phone rang. He answered it. Listened and said: "You're shitting me." Listened and said: "You're shitting me." Listened and said: "We're on our way." He hung up and looked at me. "There was an incident at a strip club in your neck of the woods."

I frowned. I certainly didn't live near any strip clubs. My only guess was: "Philly?"

Morris nodded. "A bouncer was stabbed. Guy got away. But here's the thing: Apparently there's a dancer there with one hell of an interesting story to tell."

CHAPTER 34

The strip club was in Center City, Philadelphia. Morris drove us there as if I was in labor.

"One of the responding officers is friends with one of the officers who was on the scene in Newark," he said on the drive. "Apparently they've discussed the case at length."

"And this responding officer made the connection based on the stripper's testimony?"

Morris gunned a yellow light. "Sharp kid, I guess."

"It sounds pretty thin, Tim. It could be nothing."

"Or it could be something."

My phobia theory was hardly a secret anymore. Morris and I had contemplated keeping a lid on it like the right palm, but we needed manpower, especially after what we discovered about Hal Redmond's fear of fire and the West Chester student's fear of dogs. Word travels fast—and when you're no longer trying to keep a lid on things, it can be a blessing.

"So this drunken patron we hope is our guy just up and spilled his guts?" I asked.

"Enough for the officer on the scene to think it might be significant. Not to mention the description the stripper gave was damn close to the one the waitress at the coffee place gave us."

"Jesus, maybe you were right," I said. "Maybe he *did* screw up."

"We can only hope."

That's the way it worked sometimes. Cool as it would be to track your man all the way to his front door, more often than not, you just got lucky. One of Dahmer's would-be victims escaped and led police straight back to Dahmer's apartment. Joel Rifkin got picked up for driving without plates, with a body in the back of his truck.

"What exactly did the stripper say?" I asked.

Morris cut in front of a Buick, and the driver laid on his horn. "That's what we're going to find out."

CHAPTER 35

The Cherry Club was down an alley off Chancellor Street. Probably would have been tough to find had it not been for all the black and whites flashing out front. Morris showed his credentials, and we went inside.

The club was like a cave after stepping in from the afternoon sun. It smelled like smoke, sweat, and body spray. I was grateful my senses from the drug were not particularly acute at the moment; an intense snoot full of all of the above—or, God forbid in such a place, a snoot full of something else—would have been unbearable.

The only remaining people inside the club were employees and a few patrons being interviewed by local PD. One in a group of officers in back spotted Morris and me and waved us over.

·   ·   ·

"Agent Morris? I'm Detective Dandridge." He then gestured to the other two. "Officers Howe and Carter."

We did our hellos.

Detective Dandridge, tall and very thin with silver hair and serious bags under his eyes, waved over a dancer who was standing in the corner with a female officer. The dancer was smoking a cigarette and looking both rattled and angry. The female officer brought her to us.

"This is Crystal," Dandridge said. "She was the dancer who was with your guy."

"Not sure he's our guy yet," Morris said. "We hope so."

Dandridge nodded. "She gave us everything, but I figured you'd want to hear it for yourself. She scratched him pretty good. We found blood under one of her nails. Already sent it off with orders to step on it. Fingers crossed for a hit. You got everything you need?"

Morris smiled. "For now, yeah. Thanks, Detective."

Dandridge nodded again. "Bartender over there served him—" He gestured towards the bar where two officers stood talking to a woman. "Might wanna talk to her as well."

Morris smiled and thanked him again.

Dandridge left, the remaining officers following behind. Just me, Morris, and Crystal now.

*　　　*　　　*

Crystal lit another cigarette. She inhaled and exhaled with force, as if each drag was a curse on the guy who'd attacked her.

"I knew he was drunk," she said, "but, you know—a lot of them are."

"Did he say anything before he started getting grabby?" I asked.

She exhaled hard, a short, fast stream. "Kept going on about being a real man, and that he was no 'pussy mama's boy,' whatever the hell that means." She snorted. "He even made me repeat it to him. Fucking psycho is what he was."

"What else did he say?" I asked.

"Said he wasn't afraid of anything. Then he tried to lick my tits." Another hard and fast inhale and exhale.

Morris and I exchanged glances.

"What happened after that?" Morris asked. "After he tried to lick you?"

"I told him not to. I was polite though. It happens."

"Did he get angry?"

She thought about it for a second. "Not at first. He seemed more frustrated than angry."

"How so?"

"He kept trying to touch my tits. Kept telling me it was okay because he wasn't afraid anymore. Then—and the detective said you'd think this was important—he said those *other guys* were afraid, but *he* wasn't."

If I hadn't known Morris so well, I would've said he remained stone. But I did know him well, and for a brief moment, I saw hope tease the forever stress lines etched on his face.

"Did he elaborate in any way?" Morris asked.

She took a final drag of her cigarette and dropped it to the floor where she stubbed it out with the toe of a high heel. "It was hard to tell; he was hammered. Kept slurring his words and repeating himself. None of it made any sense to me, and I didn't really give a shit—I was just trying to finish the dance while keeping his hands off me."

"Don't suppose he gave you his name?" I asked.

She pursed her lips and gave me a look. "Don't you think I'd have told you that?"

I swallowed the urge to smack her in the head. It came out as a low grumble.

Morris spotted my annoyance and quickly said: "So you were trying to finish up the dance…"

"Yeah, but now he was starting to get angry. He grabbed hold of my ass and pulled me in real close. He started thrusting up into me and saying: 'Not anymore, not anymore…'"

Morris frowned. "What do you think he meant by that?"

She shrugged. "No idea."

I got back in the game. "Is that when you started to fight him off?"

"Yup. I tried pushing myself off, but he only held on tighter. And now he was getting really worked up, saying: '*Don't need you anymore, bitch. Don't need you anymore, bitch.*'"

Morris's frown furrowed deeper. "And you have no idea what he was referring to? You didn't say anything to him earlier that he might have been alluding to?"

She looked away in thought for a moment, then slowly started shaking her head. "No…no, sorry."

"All right, then what?" I asked.

"I started hitting him. Scratching, clawing, going for his eyes…"

"Did he fight back?" Morris asked.

"Only when I called him a freak."

Morris asked her to elaborate.

"I called him a freak and told him to let go. That's when he grabbed me by the throat and started choking me. He was on top of me screaming that 'they' were the freaks, not him. Then he started screaming 'not anymore' again and again. I swear I was about to black out, but Anthony came in and pulled him off."

"The bouncer," Morris said.

She nodded. "Yeah. He, uh…" She looked away as though upset. "He, uh…he had hold of the guy by the neck, and I guess I was so angry that I got up and started to attack him while Anthony had a hold of him."

"That's understandable," Morris said.

"Yeah, but he had to toss the freak aside to control me." She was clearly upset now. "I didn't mean for it to—I mean if I had known…they usually frisk you at the door."

"Are you saying while Anthony was restraining you, the guy pulled a knife and stabbed Anthony?"

She looked away, frowning away tears. She lit another cigarette and dragged hard on it. "Asshole freak," she muttered.

"Reports we got are that Anthony's going to be okay," Morris said.

Still looking away, Crystal began nodding nervously. "Thank God."

"So he took off after?" Morris said, reaching into his breast pocket.

"Like a bolt," she said.

Morris unfolded a square of paper he'd pulled from his pocket. It was the composite sketch of our guy. He showed it to her.

"That could be him," she said. "I mean, it's a drawing, but it does kinda look like him."

Morris kept the sketch in her face. "Would you change anything on it, you think?" he asked. "If we had an artist come in who could touch the sketch up, would you change anything? Nothing is too small."

She studied the sketch again and then slowly began to shake her head, eyes staying on the paper as she spoke. "No...no, it's pretty good. I wouldn't change anything."

Morris thanked her and put the sketch away, hope still taunting his cynicism.

"Who is this guy anyway?" she asked.

"Just someone we're looking for," Morris said.

"Well, I hope you catch the asshole."

"You scratched him good?" Morris asked.

"Damn right."

Morris smiled. "Well, then that'll help. Not many places a guy with a mark like that on his face can hide, never mind his DNA."

Crystal actually smiled back. A flirty smile, no less. Then, I kid you not, she made Morris blush (just a teensy bit, but no *way* was it hiding from me) when she said: "It was my pleasure, Officer. You come back, and you've got a private dance on me."

I was about to tell her it was "agent," not "officer," but Morris looked as if he didn't give two poops, so I let his ego bask.

Still, ever the professional, Morris held up a hand and offered a polite smile. "Thank you."

Crystal suddenly gestured to the hand Morris had raised to decline her offer. "I just remembered something," she said. "He kept saying 'not anymore' over and over, but he only started saying it *after* he showed me his palm."

Morris's eyebrows bounced. "What?"

"Yeah—he showed me his palm and said, '*See this? Not anymore.*'" She re-enacted the scene with her own palm as she spoke. "It had this thick scar on it. Yeah, I remember exactly now—he showed me a scar on his palm and said: '*You see this? Not anymore, not anymore.*'"

"Was it his right palm?" I asked.

"Yeah, I think it was."

CHAPTER 36

Morris had asked me to interview the bartender while he gave the composite sketch to local PD with the new info that our guy was likely sporting a decent scratch or two on his face thanks to Morris's new girlfriend, Crystal (if he thought I wasn't going to bring that up again, he was nuts).

Unfortunately, too much time had passed between the incident and our arrival to set up any decent roadblocks. The guy was probably two states over by now, but by all accounts, he was also drunk. This meant, if he had a brain in his head, public transportation, but then our brains are typically on hiatus when we're drunk, so it was possible he could have jumped into a car and drove himself.

Still, transit police got their APBs; cabbies got word to keep an eye out for drunken fares matching our guy's description; hotels and motels got private bulletins in case he decided to crash and lay low; and, just in case our guy's drunken brain *was* on hiatus and he did decide to get behind the wheel, Morris organized patrol on all state borders. Our guy had already screwed up big-time, and with any luck, *his* luck would continue to plummet. Morris was amped, and he had a right to be. We were close.

.　　.　　.

The bartender didn't give me anything too useful. She too had identified him from the sketch and said he'd started drinking heavily shortly after his arrival. She'd said he seemed upset about something, pounding the bar with his fist at one point. Soon after was when he'd started drinking heavily, switching from gin and tonics to straight gin. She said he loosened up not long after and began to get friendly.

What had gotten him so upset? I wondered. His new moniker? "High Striker" was indeed lame, but I'd heard lamer. No, I doubted that was it. Our guy didn't seem the type to bask in the limelight. He was no BTK or Happy Face Killer; he wanted anonymity to keep doing his thing. My gut told me he'd had a setback of some kind. If my burgeoning profile on this guy was correct, my guess was that he'd been emasculated somehow.

How, though? And by whom?

.　　.　　.

When I met Morris outside, the afternoon sun after the gloom of the bar forced me to squint.

"Bartender give you anything?" he asked.

"Said he was visibly upset when he arrived. Started drinking heavily after."

"Strip club in Philadelphia," he said. "Good chance he lives here."

I thought of the guy sharing my city. I didn't like it.

"Thoughts on what Crystal said?" Morris asked.

"About giving you a free dance?"

He ignored that. "About the guy's right palm being scarred. Any thoughts?"

"Not yet."

"'Not *anymore*' she claims he said after showing her his palm. What the hell does that mean?"

"I don't know. Like I said to you before, we might never know, at least until he's caught. And if we do find out, it will almost assuredly be disappointing."

"Come again?"

"Why his palm is scarred? Why he injures the palms of his victims? It will be a letdown when we find out. It always is. The reasons are his—something personal to him. To the rest of us it'll probably result in a unanimous chorus of '*Is that it?*'"

"What are you doing?" Morris said, annoyed.

"I'm just saying it's not gonna be some epic reveal that explains all the world's evil. They're never the monsters the media paints them to be. No horns, no tails, no fangs. Just sick pathetic men you wouldn't glance twice at on the street."

"You ready to come down from your pedestal now?" Morris said. "Start telling me stuff I *don't* know?"

"You're the one who wanted my thoughts. I gave you what was in my head."

"Well maybe your head can cook a little longer on it. Or better yet, start pulling out some of your voodoo magic." He cast me what felt like accusatory eyes. "You haven't been doing much of it lately."

"Oh geez, I'm sorry, Tim—I'll try harder."

He pursed his lips at my sarcasm. "Whatever. I'm just saying that you were a human sponge when we started. What's changed?"

"Nothing has changed. The drug is the same stupid enigma it's always been." A thought then occurred to me. "Maybe the side effects are waning."

"Huh?"

"It happens with some drugs—initial side effects dissipate over time with continued use."

"So then what—you need to take *more*?"

"Yeah, that's it. If I can get my blood pressure up to a coke fiend's, then no evildoer is safe—assuming I can pause long enough between bathroom breaks to catch them."

He dropped his head and nodded a silent apology.

I started for the car.

"Where are you going?" he asked.

I stopped at the passenger door. "Did you want to hang outside a seedy strip club all day?"

We pulled into traffic and headed south.

CHAPTER 37

We didn't stray too far, deciding instead to kill time up and down Philadelphia's renowned South Street, a mosaic of unique shops, restaurants, and bars.

Morris was relatively quiet the entire time, his churning mind pinching his tongue. I couldn't blame him. We were close. Our guy had been dumping bodies up and down the entire East Coast, and here we were, smack in the city he'd just been in not more than a few hours ago. There was that paradoxical feeling of both hope and frustration that every member of law enforcement has felt at one time or another. It felt like a game of pin the tail on the donkey. You knew the damn donkey was in the room, but the blindfold prevented you from pinning the tail smack on his butt. What we wouldn't give to be able to peek.

·   ·   ·

Morris was in a bookstore, two shops down. I was in a quaint antique shop that smelled of old wood and polish. A beautiful little music box caught my eye. It was small and silver, tarnished from age. The price tag was not kind, and I hesitated picking it up for fear of breaking and, thus, buying it. Curiosity for its tune got the better of me, and I gently placed the silver box in my palm and opened the delicate lid.

I recognized the tune instantly. "All the Pretty Little Horses." A bitter wave of nostalgia washed over me. My father coming home drunk, deciding to take his frustrations out on both my mother *and* me that night. My mother taking me in her arms after it was over, her face swelling by the second from my father's hands, my bottom raw from his belt. My mother then singing to me in the most nurturing of tones despite her pain, rocking me gently on the bed as I cried into her chest—

"You break it, you bought it." A male voice behind me, throwing both a warning and a lifeline, rescuing me from my past.

I came to and spun. The shopkeeper, an old and miserable-looking man who seemed out of place in the store's quaint serenity.

"Huh?"

The shopkeeper's scowl dropped towards my hand, now a fist, the tiny box inside it and being squeezed without my realizing.

"*Oh!*" I said and immediately opened my hand. Before I could help it, the box dropped to the wooden floor with a dull clatter. The music stopped.

The shopkeeper's gaze fell with the box. When he looked back up at me, his scowl was a greedy smirk. "Cash or credit?" he said. "No personal checks."

.   .   .

"What do you have there?" Morris asked as we met on the street between the bookstore and the antique shop.

I held up the small felt bag containing the pricey music box and said: "Ramen noodles for the next month. You?"

Morris held up a paper bag the size of a large book. "*Moby Dick*. First-edition hardcover."

"Pants on fire."

He sighed and pulled the book from his bag and waved it at me. I didn't catch the title, but there was a baseball player on the front of it.

I smiled and gestured to his hip where he kept his phone. "Anything yet?"

"No. Wanna grab a bite?"

I'd forgotten how much Morris liked to eat. Apparently Chinese food and a hot dog hadn't been enough. I was still full from lunch, and my pleasant little flashback in the antique store wasn't helping my appetite any.

"Not hungry," I said.

"Wanna watch me eat?"

"Oh, yes, please."

We headed towards a café in the distance. My palm was sore from squeezing the music box, and I rubbed it along the way.

CHAPTER 38

The outdoor section of the café was noisy with street traffic, so when Morris got a call from our SAC, he slapped a hand over one ear and hurried inside, leaving his sandwich and baseball book on the table.

I sat waiting, turning my newly acquired music box over and over in my hand. I would not open it, even to check and see whether it *had* truly broken when I'd dropped it to the floor. I'm not even sure why I bought it. I could have easily told the guy to piss off, pulled rank if I had to, but I suppose I was rattled from the whole experience and complied the way a child would. A fitting analogy, I suppose, as I'd just returned from a trip to my childhood.

A weird part of me wanted to have the box…so that no one else could. Like obtaining some deadly artifact and locking it away so it couldn't hurt anyone. Silly, I know, but when has life ever made any damn sense when it comes to coping with our demons?

Open it…just to see if you really broke it or not.

No. I know the song.

So you're never going to open it?

No.

Then get rid of it.

No.

You're being ridiculous. Meet it head on, Maggie.

I set the box on the table and stared at it as though it were alive, able to jump at me on a moment's notice.

Are you past your childhood?

Yes.

And yet the box remains closed. Keeping it closed says you're not past anything.

Just because I'm past it doesn't mean I enjoy revisiting.

Are you worried that once it's open, it will remain open? That the past demons will infect current demons, make them that much stronger?

All demons interact; it's unavoidable.

Yes, but not all people use those demons to their advantage, to strengthen themselves as you have. Your abusive father made you tough; the loss of your husband and son led you here, searching for a killer. You're stronger than you think. Open the damn box and prove it, Maggie.

God, I annoy myself.

I snatched the box and opened it, anything but gentle. There was no music. I *had* broken it. I closed the tiny lid and placed it back on the table.

I suppose that was meant to be cathartic?

Do you feel better?

I exhaled long and slow through puffed cheeks.

A little.

What would make it a lot?

If Morris came back to the table and told me they picked our guy up in New Jersey somewhere.

Morris came back to the table. He did *not* look as if they just picked up our guy in New Jersey somewhere.

"What'd they say?" I asked.

"No hits from the sketch in West Chester. He must have courted the kid strictly online and then abducted him after they met at the coffee shop...or later, I don't know." He was struggling to hide his frustration.

"What else?" I asked.

"No ID on the guy in upstate PA yet. Jesus, how long has it been? Guy must have been a recluse."

"Not too surprising," I said. "A crippling phobia is likely to keep more people indoors than out. Could have been agoraphobic too for all we know."

Morris snorted. "For all we know."

"What else?" I asked.

"Pulled up nothing in the net we cast," he said.

I chuckled. "It's seriously early days, Tim."

"He's drunk, wounded, and totally flustered. Should have gotten something by now."

"You can't be serious, Tim. For all we know he's hiding in a dumpster in an alley somewhere. Or maybe he even lives here like you said. He wouldn't have far to go if that's the case, and he'd know the area well enough to stay low and out of sight."

"We're so goddamn close," he said, running a hand through his hair.

"Yes, we are. Don't start getting flustered. You were optimistic—for you anyway—not a few hours ago."

Morris grumbled and started gnawing on his thumbnail.

"You're being silly," I said.

He took his thumbnail out of his mouth. "How's that?"

"I don't need to tell you."

"I'm as human as the next person. I'm allowed to get frustrated."

"Except now is the time when you should be *least* frustrated. We've got a lot going for us. DNA could come back with a hit; there's a good chance he's in the system for lesser crimes when he was escalating. The net you cast is still very sticky; it could turn up something. And someone *will* eventually identify John Doe in upstate PA."

"The West Chester trip was a bust," he said, refusing to take off his half-empty filter.

"No it wasn't. We confirmed the kid had a phobia. The waitress at the coffee shop gave us a solid sketch; the dancer only needed a few seconds with it to recognize our guy. The waitress also gave us some damn good insight into our guy's psyche with his behavior in the shop."

"And it gave us what?" he said. "Really, at the end of the day, what did it give us? We're sitting here now because the guy screwed up. That's all. If the net catches him, it's because we got lucky."

"And you won't take that?" I let out an incredulous little laugh. "You better get your wish list in order, buddy. Not too long ago you said you'd like it if our guy got careless like Dahmer or Bundy. Now you're saying that's not good enough?"

"It feels like a cheap win."

"It's a win. Sometimes we catch them red-handed, and sometimes we get lucky."

I wasn't telling Morris anything he didn't already know. But sometimes that's how it worked. No matter how seasoned the listener might be, sometimes they needed to be reminded of the stinking obvious when frustration made you deaf to it all. And we'd all been there. Sometimes you gave the speech, sometimes you heard it.

Morris began gnawing on his thumbnail again.

"Tim, you're getting weird on me. Would you please relax? Sit down and eat your sandwich."

"He screwed up," he said. "We thought he was too careful, but he screwed up, and now we can't make him pay for it?"

"Of course we can. But come on, it's been what—a few *hours*? Sit down and eat or I'm calling your mother."

Fittingly, Morris took a seat and began poking his sandwich with a distrustful finger like a child.

"I thought you were hungry," I said.

"I was," he said, still poking.

Morris's phone rang again, and once again he slapped a hand over his ear and hurried inside the café.

.   .   .

When Morris returned, he looked a hell of a lot better than he had before. Eager. I didn't need to ask; he started talking immediately.

"Wilmington PD got something on the first victim. They got around to following up on the phobia angle and visited the guy's wife. She claimed her husband had a constant fear of his father stemming from childhood."

I could relate.

Morris went on.

"So it turns out the guy's father recently passed, and it's a trigger. Suddenly the guy is drinking too much, sudden outbursts, missing work—all kinds of erratic behavior. His wife begs him to get help, but he refuses. They start fighting constantly. Soon the guy is going out for hours at a time, and his wife thinks their constant arguing is pushing him into the arms of another woman. So she starts snooping, and lo and behold, there's a phone number tucked away in his wallet. But here's the thing: She never called it. The poor guy gets murdered by our guy soon after, and she's thinking that if her husband *was* having an affair, she doesn't want to know about it—now that he's gone, she'd rather go on thinking he'd been faithful, doesn't want to tarnish her memory of him, et cetera, et cetera."

"But she kept the number?" I asked.

"But she kept the number," he said. "Maybe she was planning to call it one day, I don't know, but she kept it."

"And?"

"Wilmington PD called it. Turned out to be a number to a support group. He *was* seeking help. He was keeping it a secret for whatever reason, but he *was* seeking help. Are you ready for the punch line?"

I nodded impatiently.

"The support group? It's run by your buddy, Dr. Cole."

CHAPTER 39

Stupid, stupid, stupid.

How could he have been so goddamn stupid? One little setback and he gets wasted and—oh *GOD*, what had he said? What had he told the stripper? Did he tell her who he was?

Who he *really* was?

"The High Striker," as the media so ludicrously called him? (Though a part of him would have to confess, he *did* like the nation-wide dread the moniker was instilling in people. The power.)

He racked his still-slightly-drunken brain, desperate to snatch at any fuzzy snippet that could prove telling. Nothing solid was forthcoming; his conversation with the stripper—did he even re-member her name? Candy? Cat?—was buried deep beneath the stabbing incident. Adrenaline had momentarily sobered him to re-call *those* events.

He'd stabbed someone.

In public.

His only saving grace was the dimness of the club, his running for the door. There was a chance no one got a good look except for the stripper and the bouncer. And the stripper saw *how many* pa-trons a night? The bouncer too? There was a good chance his face was blurred with a dozen others, wasn't there?

But then she'd scratched him. Scratched him good, the bitch. They would be looking for a man with a sizable scratch on his face now.

He looked into his bathroom mirror. Yes, it was a good one—a few inches long, right across his left cheek. It would sting when he sobered up.

What now? Oh God, what now? The police had undoubtedly shown up after he'd fled. They would be looking for him. They'd always been looking for him, of course, but he'd always been so careful before.

He'd screwed up big-time.

What to do? Run and hide? For how long, though? He'd worked too damn hard just to toss it all aside. He'd come too far.

He needed to regroup. He'd screwed up, and he needed to regroup. All was not lost. Dammit, all was *not* lost. It couldn't be. He wouldn't let it. He had to get it back. Get the feeling back. Reclaim what he'd worked so hard for.

He hurried out of the bathroom and went straight for his safe. He screwed up the combination on the first two tries, his dexterity sloppy with anticipation and alcohol.

The third try was a success. He opened the safe and removed the DVD album. Inside that album was his whole world, the brilliant result of all his hard work. Six of them, to be exact. Six disks for six brilliant results.

But which to choose? Each was special in its own unique way; all of them were empowering.

Empowering.

That's what he needed now more than anything. To feel empowered again. To know and believe—*truly believe*—that one little setback was not, was *not*, was NOT going to undo all he'd done.

And therefore any of them would do, would they not?

He pulled number six. The homeless man he'd found in Trenton. The one he'd taunted with fire. The disk had initially been reserved for the man in upstate Pennsylvania who was afraid of being buried alive. God, he'd prepared so long for that one. How great it would have been if it had come to fruition. But the homeless man from Trenton had proved a decent consolation prize. Such a tough man brought to his knees in a pleading, quivering mess from a little fire. A decent consolation prize indeed, but it was still fresh in his memory. He placed number six aside.

He pulled number five. The student from West Chester University. Afraid of dogs. He'd never heard a man screech like that before. It had an alien quality to it, as if his vocal cords had transcended all capable pitches of the human body. When the kid had passed out for the third time, he took a selfie with the unconscious boy and one of the dogs. But this too was still reasonably fresh. And he could always look at the selfie.

Number four. The black man from Maryland. Afraid of spiders. How many pet stores in how many towns had he visited in preparation? At least two dozen? He'd ended up with nearly fifty of the big hairy buggers, buying only two at a store so as not to raise suspicion, so yes, at least two dozen stores visited sounded about right. The black man was the only one who managed to puke, shit, and piss at the same time. Now *that* was funny. But no, he didn't want that one either.

Number three. The guy from New York City. Afraid of the dark. He'd bought an infrared camera for this one. He'd kept him in the cellar of an abandoned warehouse on the outskirts of the city for three days, periodically sneaking up on him and poking him with a stick from all angles. This man—though he wasn't really a man, was he?—also screeched in alien tones whenever blindly poked and prodded. The man eventually started calling for his mother.

His *mother*.

He'd stopped recording shortly after that. He did not want to watch this one either. The mother part still bothered him. In the future, he might edit that bit out.

Number two. The older man from upstate New York. Afraid of the water. Afraid of drowning. The isolated lake he'd found had been too perfect. Though he'd gagged this one, he hadn't needed to: they were miles from anywhere. Dunk, hold, release; dunk, hold, release; and so on. How fun it had been, the pleading terror in the man's eyes, so enormous in compensation for his inability to beg while gagged.

He ultimately decided against number two as well.

He wanted number one. Though it had the lowest quality of all his films—he had to improvise on the spot; he hadn't planned on filming, hadn't really planned on any of it—it was perhaps nearest and dearest to his heart. The start of his journey towards change.

He placed number one into his Blu-ray and took a seat. His bladder felt full with anticipation as the Blu-ray whirred to life, about to make everything better, ready to empower him once again.

What he saw disappointed him.

He saw his first victim, cuffed and pleading and crying, asking *why?* over and over again. *They were friends*, he'd pleaded, *had established trust, divulged horrific truths about their past to one another. Why? Why? Why?*

He'd left him there in his home, only to return with a dress, insisting the man put it on, reminding him what would happen to his wife if he did not. He'd then stood over the crying "man" in a dress, berating him like he'd claimed his father had, kicking him, punching him, calling him every conceivable emasculating name he could fathom, giggling and grinning and giggling some more as he did so.

He'd even urinated on him at one point.

At the time, it had all been so wonderful. Established the blueprint for what would soon become his new life.

Now, all it did was remind him of his setback today. Remind him of who he'd once been, not who he was aspiring to be.

He stood and switched off the Blu-ray. Began pacing back and forth in his living room, desperate to reclaim the glory he'd begun to attain. His video mementos had always worked during times of doubt.

Their impact now felt negligible.

Did he need another? A new one? Yes. Definitely, yes. But he would be a fool to take one so soon after the debacle that had occurred today. He was too careful for that.

Careful! That was a laugh. He'd assaulted a stripper. Stabbed a man in public. And the stripper had scratched him good; she probably had his DNA under her fingernails.

But let's be optimistic here for one minute.

He'd never been convicted of a crime before, so he knew he wasn't in the system. And he knew he'd been so very careful at each crime scene that the odds of him leaving anything behind were minuscule.

And if the police did somehow grab him, they would only have him on assault, *maybe* attempted murder for the bouncer at the club. The things he might have said to the stripper—even if he *had* confessed to all of it in his drunkenness—could be argued away by any competent lawyer. He was wasted, he was delusional, or how about he was just plain lying?

He *did* remember showing the stripper his scarred palm. But so what? Tie a man to seven murders because he had a scar on his palm? A DA would be reprimanded for bringing such flimsiness to a judge.

The only damning evidence tying him to all seven murders was laid out here in front of him on home movies.

He would have to get rid of them. To be safe, he would have to destroy his new life's work. God forgive him, he would.

.   .   .

So he would have to start over. Yes, he needed a new one, and he would have to start over.

He could, right? There was nothing stopping him. Except time, that is—everything was too chaotic to grab someone right away.

But that was okay too. With the exception of the homeless man in Trenton, he never just grabbed someone willy-nilly. He was always meticulous with his homework, with his choosing the right one, and sometimes homework proved to be just as titillating; the anticipation for things to come was delightful foreplay.

He sat back down and collected all of his disks, gently stacking them into a neat little pile, his touch filled with both love and sorrow, an owner bidding farewell to a loyal pet before euthanasia.

Start over.

But where?

And then a thought pushed its way forward without conscious effort:

From the beginning. Start from the very beginning.

Go see Dr. Cole.

CHAPTER 40

I hung up and looked at Morris. Our new prospect with Dr. Cole and the first victim had brought his appetite back—his sandwich was nearly gone, his mouth full with a recent bite when he said: "Well?"

"He can see us first thing in the morning," I said.

Morris struggled to swallow quickly, his words impatient. "*To-morrow morning?* Why not now?"

"He's with patients all day and then running a group tonight."

"*So what?* Jesus, Mags, call him back and tell him we can't wait."

"He knows this is important, Tim, but he's not about to kick all of his patients aside at the last minute. He's loyal that way."

Morris's appetite vanished again. He pushed the rest of his sandwich away as if it now repulsed him. "This is bullshit." He pulled out his phone. "Gimme his number."

"No."

"No?"

"Show him a little respect, Tim. Dr. Cole has been extremely accommodating thus far. It would be very uncool to bully him."

"And what if he has information about the first victim that proves vital? We'll lose an entire day on it."

"Your net is cast. All conceivable bases are covered for now. We need to respect his wishes."

"And what if our guy decides to lash out and grab another one-night stand like he did the homeless guy in Trenton?" he said.

"He would have to be a complete fool to do something so reckless."

"He was drunk. A drunk man is ruled by impulses."

"If he does something stupid, then nothing Dr. Cole has on the first victim is going to prevent that. Please show Dr. Cole some respect. I wouldn't even be here helping you if it wasn't for him."

Morris looked away, my firm stance forbidding him from granting me eye contact.

When he finally looked back, he said: "Well, then I want to go to Wilmington."

"Why? Wilmington PD got all there was."

"You don't know that. I want to go to Wilmington. I don't want to just sit with my thumb up my butt until morning."

"You're being stubborn. Stick your thumb up your butt and wait."

Morris looked away again. I was actually surprised he was even considering my words—I was a "consultant," after all. He could have easily said *tough shit* and insisted we see Dr. Cole now. But maybe my history with Dr. Cole changed things. Morris knew how much I respected the good doctor.

.   .   .

Perhaps some might think I was being foolhardy by not insisting on seeing Dr. Cole today, but I stand by my reasoning, respecting his wishes being only part of it.

The second reason (among others) being that the first victim had died just under a year ago. There was a chance that Dr. Cole, when shown a photo of the first victim, wouldn't even recognize him, let alone remember what he'd said in group.

And not that Morris wasn't totally justified in his insistence. Quite often, the first victim of a serial killer is significant for many reasons, one of the big ones being the victim could have been someone the killer knew, unwittingly volunteering to be the test subject for atrocities to come.

Still, Morris's justification aside, there was the idea of bullying Dr. Cole into accommodating us after he'd been nothing *but* accommodating. You think he wanted to give me a full daily dose of the drug again? He did everything but beg me to "Just Say No," trying to endorse my God-given abilities as an investigator as an alternative rather than rely on a potentially life-threatening drug. But I, in my infinite bitch wisdom, used the poor guy's wife's murder as leverage to get the drug.

And *still* he accommodated me.

He could have immediately dropped me as a patient, told me to go eff myself for having the audacity to use his dead wife as a pawn, or just flat-out refused to give me the drug. But he didn't…because he knew it was what I wanted. And now I was going to disobey his wishes and bully him into seeing us ASAP? No way. And even if Morris did ultimately pull rank and insist, I would go kicking and screaming, if I even went at all.

* * *

Morris pushed back his chair and stood. "I waited. Now I want to go to Wilmington."

I chuckled. "We really do keep borrowing each other's demeanors, don't we?"

He frowned. "Huh?"

"Back in West Chester, when we were waiting on possible hits from support groups in the area, *I* was the one who was itching to move on to victim four and start heading to Maryland. *You* were the one who told me to let Amy Crane from the Baltimore field office do her thing and to sit tight lest we drive hundreds of unnecessary miles. *Maximum efficiency*, remember, Agent Morris, sir?"

He frowned again, my smartassery catching him like a flick on the nose. He stood there for a moment, his pride refusing to let him take a seat again.

"Fine," he eventually said. "We go in the morning. I don't agree with it, and I should remind you that *I'm*"—he tapped his index finger on his chest—"the one calling the shots, not 'the consultant'…"

Déjà vu.

"...But out of respect for your history with Dr. Cole, and because he's been so accommodating..."

Serious déjà vu.

"...I will grudgingly wait until morning."

"Thank you," I said. "Why don't you sit and finish your sandwich?"

"Stop acting like my mother."

CHAPTER 41

Morris rang my doorbell while I was still brushing my teeth. To say he looked eager would be like saying tofu was gross. He had two coffees with him, one in each hand.

"Lots of cream, no sugar, just the way you like it," he said, handing the large paper cup with the black lid to me.

"Who says men don't pay attention?" I said, taking the coffee from him and stepping away from the door to invite him in.

He stepped inside, and I closed the door behind him. I sipped my coffee—toothpaste and java. Yum.

Morris didn't stray far from the door. "You ready to go?"

I waved a hand up and down my attire—pajama bottoms and an old gray T-shirt. "Any chance I can change first?"

"Hurry up."

He'd gotten his manners out of the way by bringing me coffee; now he could be curt and impatient, guilt-free.

"I was going to take a shower," I lied.

"Maggie…"

Ugh with the *Maggie* again. "You know, when you call me Maggie, it reeks of a parent getting serious with his kid."

"Maggie, whatever you need to do, please hurry up, Maggie."

At least his impatience was not immune to a little humor.

"I don't need to shower. I just need to change."

"Then do it, Maggie."

I sipped my coffee while giving him the evil eye, then went into my bedroom and changed.

. . .

Dr. Cole's office has a waiting room and an exit room for the sake of his patients' privacy.

It was something I'd been grateful for since our very first session together. Though there is absolutely nothing wrong with seeing a psychiatrist, the stigma of doing so will exist as long as psychiatry does. Even the most tortured of individuals feeling completely just in their treatment can feel as vulnerable as if they were naked when eyes fall on them after a session, even by those waiting to be seen next.

And so Morris and I sat in Dr. Cole's waiting room...waiting. Morris was flipping through a *Sports Illustrated*, though I know he wasn't reading anything. Take the magazine away and he'd be biting his thumbnail.

I was eager myself. Though I remained steadfast in my decision to wait until this morning to see Dr. Cole, the prospect of there being something useful on the other side of his door made it difficult to think about anything else.

. . .

Dr. Cole's door opened, and he greeted us with that small but warm smile of his. "Hello, Maggie. Agent Morris..." He stepped forward with his hand extended. "Nice to see you again, under different circumstances, so to speak. Maggie's told me a lot about you since the trial."

Morris was obviously too eager for creative wit, as evidenced by his taking Dr. Cole's hand and spouting the old chestnut: "All of it good, I hope."

Dr. Cole, while no laff riot himself, earned slightly better applause with: "Oh no, not good at all."

We did the unanimous courtesy chuckle thing and stepped into Dr. Cole's office.

. . .

We all took a seat.

Dr. Cole went to speak first, but Morris beat him to it:

"I want to get this out of the way," Morris said. "Please don't give us any of that patient confidentiality nonsense—"

"*Tim.*"

Dr. Cole raised an eyebrow.

Morris went on, undeterred. "If you realize today that this killer we're looking for was a patient of yours, I'm going to insist you tell us about him. *All* about him. Are we clear on that?"

Dr. Cole calmly and politely responded with: "Agent Morris, I'm sure I don't have to tell you that my wife was taken from me by a serial killer. I hope that answers your question."

Morris looked both satisfied and a little guilty. Perhaps he was expecting cooperation, but not with the subject-over impact Dr. Cole had delivered it with.

"It does," Morris said. "I'm sorry if I came across a little—"

Dr. Cole held up a hand, cutting Morris off. "Forget it. Shall we proceed?"

Morris nodded. I felt like kicking him.

. . .

We started off by telling Dr. Cole all about the incident at the strip club, the possibility that our guy might actually live in Philadelphia, a copy of the composite sketch (Dr. Cole didn't recognize him). While this information wasn't necessarily pertinent to our visit with Dr. Cole, it was a decent icebreaker after Morris's sledgehammer courtesy at the start.

When the ice felt sufficiently broken, we dove right in with the pending stuff and showed Dr. Cole photos of the first victim from Wilmington.

And he recognized him.

Recognized him well, thank God.

"I never saw him privately," Dr. Cole said. "Quite often, a patient will come to me for private sessions first before I suggest attending group as adjunct therapy to their treatment. This man—what did you say his name was?"

"Alex Stern," I said.

"Alex Stern—I don't remember the alias he used in group; everybody uses one—was very active in group. Almost from the start. That's very uncommon. Likely the reason I remember him as well as I do."

"Wilmington PD contacted you yesterday," Morris said. "Were you able to dig up any notes on him?"

"I don't take notes in group," Dr. Cole said. "The primary benefit of group is for the patient to share with his or her peers, to receive support from them. I'm there strictly as an overseer, not to offer critical analysis for each patient."

"But you do remember him?" Morris asked.

"Yes. His childhood was horrific. His father was an exceptional bully and domineering man. Alex Stern was apparently frail as a child, shying away from confrontation and contact sports and the like. The father resented this and beat the boy unmercifully. I recall one session where Alex Stern confessed that his father made him wear a dress to school. He referred to his son as the daughter he never wanted."

"Jesus," Morris said. He looked at me. "You thought your father was bad."

I didn't respond. I was too preoccupied with a possible parallel beginning to form between the first victim and the killer.

"So his phobia was his father?" Morris asked. "His childhood? Is that even considered a phobia?"

"Phobias were just *one* of the things we treated in group," Dr. Cole said.

"So it doesn't fit," Morris said.

"Sure it does," I said. "If the profile on our guy is correct, he likely saw Alex Stern as a reflection of himself."

"So you're saying our guy attended the same group as Alex Stern?" Morris said.

"I'd have to say yes," I said. "Wouldn't you?"

"But it's still not a phobia," Morris said. "It still doesn't make sense how he would graduate from destroying a reflection of himself to exploiting men's fears. And let's not forget our guy's ritual—Alex Stern was cuffed and bludgeoned like all the others. His right palm damaged. Our guy's first one would be sloppier, less organized."

"Unless he got it right the first time," I said. "Bear with me for a second here. Let me paint a picture."

"Go," Morris said.

Dr. Cole looked on.

"Our guy hears about Dr. Cole's group—"

"How?" Morris broke in.

I gave him a look.

He held up an apologetic hand. "Continue."

"Our guy hears about Dr. Cole's group. I don't know how, but he does. He goes to the group, maybe with the intention of getting legitimate help. He sits and listens while people take turns spilling their guts.

"One guy gets up—Alex Stern—and according to Dr. Cole, he isn't shy about opening up. He talks about his horrific childhood and the terrible things his father did, but more importantly, as it potentially relates to our guy, how disgusted his father was with him for being weak, both physically and emotionally." I turned to Dr. Cole. "Did Alex Stern ever mention his mother?"

Dr. Cole thought for a moment. "If he did, I don't recall. My guess would be, as is common in environments with such a strong patriarchal structure, was that she was there but she wasn't, if that makes sense. Likely, she would only offer support to the child when it was safe to, when her husband was momentarily gone."

Dr. Cole's eyes clicked solely on me after these last words. I frowned back at him as if to say: *I don't have an appointment this morning, thank you.* His eyes returned to us both equally.

"Okay, I'll buy all that," Morris said to Dr. Cole. Then to me: "Why'd you ask about the mother?"

"Something the stripper said. She stated that when our guy was assaulting her, he kept repeating, 'Don't need you anymore, bitch.'

He could have been referring to his mother. Perhaps his mother consoled him after his own father's abuse."

"If she consoled him, why would he resent her?" Morris asked.

"Could be any number of things," Dr. Cole said. "Perhaps he blames his mother for sticking with his father despite his abusive behavior. But, judging from what you claim the dancer said, it sounds as though he blames his mother for enabling him to feel sorry for himself—that it was okay to be weak. Obviously this logic is absurd, but then we're not dealing with a man who shuns the absurd, are we?"

Morris grunted and then looked at me again. "Keep going, Mags."

"Okay—so let's say Alex Stern spills his guts to the group, and it hits way too close to home for our guy. Maybe at first he sees an ally in Stern, someone to talk to. Maybe they start communicating outside of group, establishing trust between one another. Maybe they get together one night, let's say at our guy's place. They start commiserating with one another, and our guy is filled with a sudden revulsion at the reflection of himself. He lashes out at Stern and attacks him. Stern is vulnerable and shows confusion and fear, and this fills our guy with a sense of power, like he suddenly has control over his own trauma. Maybe he then renders Stern unconscious and binds him—*cuffs* him—and continues the torment, taking delight in watching him squirm."

"You think he filmed it like the others?" Morris asked.

"Could have. He surely wouldn't have had anything prepared, but maybe he pulled out his phone, used that to record it, I don't know. Either way, he torments Stern incessantly, the feeling of power and control accelerating by the second. Stern's anguish becomes like a drug to our guy; the more Stern pleads and weeps, the higher our guy gets.

"Except it can't go on for very long. Despite the high, our guy soon can't help but see himself in Stern. All that fear and suffering—it's like a time machine with a mirror. So he snaps and has to destroy it. He goes caveman on him and beats him to death—beats *himself* to death."

"And the right palm?" Morris said.

"As I said before, it's probably something personal to him. Something that happened to him in his childhood maybe. He probably does something similar to his victims to replicate the torment he suffered, first to revel in seeing someone else endure it, and then ultimately to destroy it."

"So how did he graduate to phobias then?" Morris asked. "If he revels in this guy's childhood torment and then destroys a reflection of himself, how does he graduate to phobias from that?"

I sensed Morris knew the answers—many of the answers—to his own questions, but this was our routine, voicing it all aloud, volleying things back and forth. As much as you may think you know, hearing it aloud always helped.

"Phobias are a shortcut for him. It's the fear that gets him off. Seeing grown men crumble defuses his own fears and insecurities. What better way to reach the core of a man's dread than with a crippling phobia? He certainly wasn't going to sit in on endless group sessions, hoping to find and exploit another mirror reflection of himself—it would take forever. So he took the shortcut in phobias. And unfortunately, judging by his increasing body count, it worked just fine."

Morris looked at Dr. Cole. "What do you think, Dr. Cole? She making any sense to you?"

"From a psychiatric standpoint, I'd say much of her analysis is very plausible," he said. "From a profiling standpoint dealing with serial predators, I'd say you're far better qualified to make that assessment than I."

"Do you remember Alex Stern being particularly chummy with anyone during those group sessions?" Morris asked. "Maybe a lot of talking during coffee breaks? Leaving or arriving together? Things like that?"

Dr. Cole looked disappointed with himself when he said: "I'm afraid I don't."

"Do you recall any other participants acting particularly odd during group sessions with Alex Stern?"

"No, I'm sorry."

"Don't suppose you film the group sessions, do you?"

"No."

Morris sighed.

"How was Alex Stern's progress in the group?" I asked. "Did you feel like he was making any?"

"It's difficult to say. When people stop showing up, it could be because they feel they've gotten better or because they feel therapy isn't helping."

"Anyone else stop showing up around the same time Stern did?" Morris asked.

"I really wouldn't know. People come in and out of group fairly regularly."

Morris showed Dr. Cole the sketch of our guy again. "Familiar at *all*? Chances are more than solid he sat in on at least one of your group sessions."

Again, Dr. Cole looked disappointed with himself. "Even if he did look familiar—and I'm sorry, he doesn't—I can't imagine it would help in any way. All group participants use an alias; with the exception of those who come see me first, I never know any of their real names."

"Is it possible our guy saw you privately before attending group?" I asked.

Dr. Cole shifted in his seat, looking suddenly uncomfortable. "I suppose it is."

Morris, donning his asshole hat again, said: "And you wouldn't be keeping something like that from us if he had…"

Dr. Cole's look of sudden discomfort disappeared, his need to repeat himself on an issue so personal to him likely giving annoyance the go-ahead to kick discomfort to the curb.

"No, Agent Morris, I would not. I can assure you that if I recalled treating a man who matched the descriptions we've covered, either physical or psychological, I would happily divulge them to you. As it happens, I do not."

Morris was persistent. "Maybe you could check patient files?"

"When would you like me to start checking?"

"Now."

Dr. Cole took a long blink. "What *date*, Agent?"

Morris looked at me. "I don't know—I guess a year ago, right?"

I looked away.

"What?" Morris said.

I brought my gaze back on him. "You're reaching again."

"How the hell am I reaching?" He turned to Dr. Cole. "Is it such a great effort to check your patient files from a year ago?"

"Of course not."

"Tim, stop," I said.

"Stop? Suppose our guy was a private patient before he attended group. He'd have to fill out some paperwork first, right?" He looked at Dr. Cole. "*Right?* That's standard, isn't it? Address, medical history, health insurance...?"

"*Tim.*"

"What? *What?* Goddammit, did we just come here to add more to the profile or actually take a physical step forward?"

Once again, Morris and I were swapping stances. It was almost silly by now to think either one of us was committed to a particular method of pursuit. The only unanimous thing we consistently shared was our need to catch the bastard.

"Dr. Cole would remember anyone fitting our description, Tim," I said. "He said he doesn't."

"How can it hurt to check? It's possible he forgot." He looked at Dr. Cole. "You can't remember *everyone*, right?"

"I would be happy to go through all of my patient profiles for the past *two* years," Dr. Cole said politely. "If I come across anything significant, I can have it for you by the end of the day. Does that work?"

Morris looked at me, not Dr. Cole, when he said: "That would be very helpful. Thank you."

"And if he does find something?" I said to Morris. "What will you do?"

"*What?*" Morris looked as though I'd asked him if he wanted to have my baby.

"Let's say Dr. Cole goes into his files and pulls one that is uncanny; damn good chance it's our guy. What would you do?"

"I'd pay him one hell of a visit," Morris said.

"On what grounds?"

"How about the scene he caused at the strip club? We get the stripper to ID him; we get his DNA; *boom*."

"For what? Attacking a stripper? Assaulting a bouncer? We want him for murder."

Morris frowned hard. "We get the waitress at the coffee shop to ID him too. He was one of the last people to be seen with the West Chester student."

"We don't know that for sure. We don't *have* an exact time on when he abducted that student."

"Well, all of the above would at least give us enough for a warrant to search his place."

"And if we find nothing? He'll then know we're on to him—maybe he disappears for good."

"Not if we keep an eye on him."

"For how long?"

Morris's frown was now his whole face. "*Do you want to catch him or not?*"

"I do," I said. "And if Dr. Cole does pull that uncanny file, I *would* want to keep an eye on him, but not with him knowing about it. And I don't want to settle for a simple assault charge in a strip club. I want to get the asshole for each and every brutal act of torture and murder he committed."

Morris waved a dejected hand at me and looked away. "Ah, it's all hearsay anyway," he said. "Dr. Cole might not find a thing in his files."

"My point still stands though, Tim. We want him on murder, not assault."

Morris was deflating by the second. "What about all the stuff he said to the stripper? Showing her his palm and all?"

I pursed my lips. "Come on, Tim, you know that's got weak legs."

"Well, then why the hell did we move heaven and earth casting a net to catch him after what he did at the strip club? If we'd gotten him—and we still might—we'd only have him on the assault charges anyway."

"We *had* to; he'd just stabbed a man."

"But we didn't do it in hopes of catching a man who'd just stabbed someone; we did it in hopes of getting our guy."

"He was drunk and on the run. If we *had* caught him and leaned on him hard enough, who knows what his addled brain might have confessed to?"

.   .   .

Morris went quiet for a moment, no doubt grudgingly swallowing what I'd fed him. I said it before: No matter how seasoned the listener might be, sometimes they need to be reminded of the stinking obvious when frustration made you deaf to it all.

Finally, Morris said: "So Dr. Cole pulls the uncanny file, we all but know for certain it's our guy, and all we'll do is watch and wait for him to kill again."

"We don't necessarily have to wait," I said.

Morris gave a dry chuckle. "Set a trap, right?"

I shrugged and tried to appeal to Morris with a cheesy metaphor. "A fisherman doesn't sit and wait for the fish to jump in his boat."

Morris wasn't having any of it. He just stood and extended his hand towards Dr. Cole. "Thanks again," he said.

Dr. Cole stood, and they shook hands. "My pleasure. I hope I was of some help to you both."

Now I stood. "You were. Thank you, Dr. Cole. We really appreciate you making time for us."

"Of course." He led us to the door that emptied out into his exit room. "I'll be in touch if I find anything in my patient files," he said again.

Morris handed Dr. Cole a card with our number. Dr. Cole waved it off and held up his cell phone. "I have Maggie in here," he said.

Morris nodded and put the card away.

We thanked him again and left.

.   .   .

Dr. Cole would later tell me that after escorting us out, he'd opened the door leading into his waiting room to greet his next patient.

The patient—a new patient—was already there. He would tell me his new patient was rocking back and forth in his chair, palpably anxious. Then he would tell me that this patient had looked oddly familiar and had a large bandage covering his left cheek.

CHAPTER 42

Joe Pierce sat in Dr. Cole's waiting room, anxious to get started. This would be the first step in starting over.

He could have gone straight to group like he'd done the last time, but it was too soon for group. Too risky. Still, he couldn't wait. If he couldn't attend group, he could do the next best thing.

He wasn't really sure what he was going to tell Dr. Cole; he certainly wasn't going to tell him who he was or what he'd done. What he wanted was to lay some groundwork. *Ask* about group—what kind of people were currently attending, what issues were being covered…was there anyone there worth getting excited about.

He would have to play this exceptionally cool. If he walked in there with an agenda, advertising the eagerness he felt, Dr. Cole would spot it instantly. Maybe not link him to The High Striker—how could he?—but certainly spot an ulterior motive.

.   .   .

Dr. Cole opened his office door and stepped into the waiting room. Joe stood. Dr. Cole looked different than Joe remembered. In group he appeared so calm and in control, even during the odd outburst or breakdown from a group participant.

Now he looked unsure of himself, less in control.

You were a different man back then, Joe immediately told himself. *Of course Dr. Cole looked more assured back then, and less assured now. This is what it's like when you meet up with people from your past life—they're no longer better than you.*

And the guys at the office?

Stop it. A minor setback is all it was. It was a minor setback, and you're going to start over and fix it. Fix all *of it—starting now.*

"Charlie?" Dr. Cole said with an extended hand.

Joe took his hand and shook it. "Do you remember me, Dr. Cole? I attended a few of your group sessions a while back."

Dr. Cole gave what appeared to be a quick and courteous study of Joe—a slight tilt of the head, a slight squint of the eyes. Then: "I'm sorry, I don't. Group has a very different structure than my private practice. People are always coming and going; pseudonyms; it's tough to keep track."

Joe waved a forgiving hand. "Ah, that's okay—I was a different man back then. Didn't talk much. Largely forgettable, you might say."

"What happened?" Dr. Cole asked, gesturing to Joe's face.

He'd expected this and had a reply at the ready. "Cat," he said with a smile. "Just adopted one. I guess you could say we're still getting to know one another."

Dr. Cole smiled back and stepped aside, gesturing towards his office. "Shall we?"

. . .

Seated now, Joe Pierce dove right in.

"You might be wondering why I came to you first as opposed to just going straight to group like I did before," he said.

"I'm sure you have your reasons," Dr. Cole said.

"I do."

Dr. Cole sat quietly and waited.

"I'm not sure I'm ready for group," Joe said. "I'm not sure"—*don't sound too eager*—"there would be anyone there I might be able to identify with."

"In what way?" Dr. Cole asked.

"Someone there with the same issues I have."

"Were you able to identify with anyone the last time you attended?"

Oh yeah.

"A little."

"Well, then perhaps this time will be no different."

"I guess..."

"I have no intention of pressuring you into anything, Charlie. However, it's clear your aim for our appointment today is to see whether there are any members in group with whom you could empathize."

Joe felt a sudden pang of anxiety. Dr. Cole had spotted his agenda after all.

But he'd only spotted his *surface* agenda, hadn't he? He could never know his *true* reasoning behind that agenda—that was impossible.

So just roll with it. Roll with the surface agenda. No harm in that.

"Is it that obvious?" he said, an intentional look of shame on his face.

"Obvious, yet hardly uncommon," Dr. Cole said with a reassuring smile. "Why not elaborate a bit more on the issues you mentioned? Perhaps I can tell you whether there are any group regulars you might be able to identify with."

Joe began to nod, slow and unsure at first, and then faster and more certain as he ultimately decided it harmless to give just enough.

"My father," he said. "He was a very demanding man."

"Demanding how?"

"I could never please him."

"Was he abusive?"

"Yes."

"More physical or mental?"

"Both."

"Was your mother in the picture?"

"Yes."

"Was she abusive too?"

He struggled to hide his contempt. "She might as well have been."

"I can see this is difficult for you to discuss, Charlie. I think you're correct in your assumption that it would be beneficial to listen to other members in group you can identify with to further your therapy. You'll only know, however, if you attend. We're holding one this evening."

"That's too soon." The words were out of his mouth before he could consider better phrasing.

"I'm sorry?" Dr. Cole said.

"I just meant I'm not sure if I'm ready," he said.

But oh how he was. He so was.

"I understand," Dr. Cole said. "When you *are* ready, I'm sure you'll find quite a few attendees you can relate to. In fact..." He trailed off, looking away in thought for a moment.

Joe leaned forward in his seat. "What?"

Dr. Cole came to. "Just recalling a recent member of group. He claimed to be coping with baggage quite similar to yours. I'm sorry it didn't come to me right away."

"That's okay," Joe said quickly. "What do you mean by similar baggage?"

"Domineering and abusive father. Saw his son as weak, a disappointment." Dr. Cole looked away again in recall. "I remember him saying something about his mother, how her only purpose seemed to be picking up the pieces she did nothing to prevent from breaking. His resentment for her felt touchable." Dr. Cole placed his gaze back on Joe. "Does something like that ring any identifiable bells for you, Charlie?"

Joe's eagerness hammered in his chest. He drew blood biting down on the inside of his cheek to contain it.

"Maybe a few," he managed to say.

"Still," Dr. Cole said, "you come when you're ready, Charlie. I don't want to rush you into anything. I'm sure there will be someone at group you can relate to when you feel the time is right."

"What about the guy you just mentioned? You said he was recent."

Dr. Cole began to fiddle with a clipboard, his gaze leaving Joe as he pulled a few papers from his desk and clipped them to the board. "True. But people come and go in group; I can't promise he'll be there when you feel ready to show." He handed the clipboard over. "But I'm sure someone will eventually." Dr. Cole smiled another reassuring smile.

The smile was *anything* but reassuring.

"I'm going to pay cash," Joe said flatly, handing the clipboard back to Dr. Cole as if it were an unwanted gift.

"I'd still like to have some background information on you, Charlie—if you don't mind."

"But we know I was only here to find out about group. I don't plan on coming back for private sessions."

"Okay then, Charlie." Dr. Cole set the clipboard aside. "I certainly won't make you do anything you don't want to."

.   .   .

Later that night, Dr. Cole said to the group: "I see some new faces. Would any of you like to introduce yourselves? No real names, please."

Joe Pierce raised his hand.

CHAPTER 43

Joe Pierce stood before the group—a circle of roughly thirty people, men and women, seated on folding chairs. The venue was a local high school classroom.

"My name is Tom," Joe said.

A unanimous greeting from the group.

"Hi, Tom," Dr. Cole said. "Would you like to tell us why you're here?"

Joe scanned the circle of faces, wondering whether the one Dr. Cole had mentioned this morning was in attendance.

"Sure," he said. "I guess I'm looking for support, is all."

"Support for what, Tom?"

"Childhood stuff. It's been…hitting me hard lately."

"Would you like to elaborate?"

Joe faked a hard swallow, cleared his throat as if it was all so difficult. "Yeah, um…you know…good old 'daddy' issues, I guess." He faked a nervous chuckle now. The group chuckled with him. Good.

"What about your father?" Dr. Cole asked.

"Let's just say I was a grave disappointment to him."

A man spoke up. "Why do you say that?"

All eyes immediately clicked on the man—the first member of the evening to engage another was always treated as a spectacle.

Joe turned his attention to the man. He appeared middle-aged and fit. Dark, thinning hair. His face was somber as he waited for Joe's reply.

"I had a lot of anxiety as a child," Joe said. "I guess you could say this lessened his opinion of me."

"Not tough enough?" the man asked.

Joe's chin retracted as though the man had taken a swipe at him. Without conscious thought, he replied: "Yes."

The man nodded and grunted. "I hear ya, brother," was all he said.

Joe, still a little stunned by the man's curt yet insightful inquiry, could only nod in thanks for the support.

"Do you feel up to elaborating a little more, Tom?" Dr. Cole asked. Then to the man who'd spoken up: "Or you perhaps?"

The man shrugged. *Sure, why not?* his shrug said. He stood. "My name's Bob."

Unanimous hellos.

"Like Tom over there, I was a disappointment to my father."

Joe remained standing as he listened. Was this him?

"Why do you think you were a disappointment to your father?" Dr. Cole asked.

"I don't have to think; *I know*. He had no problem telling me or showing me." Bob gave a humorless chuckle. The group recognized it and did not return an accommodating chuckle as they had for Joe.

"My dad was a football star in college until he tore his ACL," Bob went on. "Hopes and dreams gone. I guess the next best thing after that was a kid he could live vicariously through. Except I was frail as a kid. Not one for sports." Bob shrugged again, perhaps hoping the group could fill in the blanks from there.

Joe needed more. "What did he do?" he asked.

Bob frowned. "What do you mean?"

"I don't know...what were some of the things he did to show you his disappointment?"

"He beat the shit out of me," Bob said.

"Language, please," Dr. Cole said.

Bob held up an apologetic hand. He then brought his attention back to Joe.

"He liked to drink," he said. "One night he came home with all this little league football equipment. He insisted I put it on and then moved all of the furniture in the living room. He made my mother hike me the ball, and then he would tackle me. He knocked me cold on the first hit. I was probably ninety pounds at the time."

There were a few sympathetic murmurs from the group. Bob went on.

"My mother wanted to take me to the hospital, but he refused. When she insisted, he granted her wish—except she ended up going alone, if you know what I mean."

More sympathetic murmurs.

"Did your mother ever tell anyone?" Joe asked.

Bob barked out a laugh. "*Hell* no."

There was an awkward pause.

"What is it you're hoping to get from group, Bob?" Dr. Cole asked.

Bob shrugged once again. "I'm not really sure. I thought I'd moved past it all, you know? I have my own family now, a good life. I'm not frail anymore—" He held up his arm, pretending to flex his bicep. The group knew to chuckle this time. "But every time I look in the mirror…"

"You see the frail boy staring back," Dr. Cole said.

Bob gave a sullen nod. "The nightmares are the worst. It's funny how the realest dreams are the ones you don't want."

This time the group murmured in understanding.

"Thanks for sharing, Bob." Then to Joe: "You too, Tom."

.   .   .

Coffee break.

Joe approached Bob, who was filling a Styrofoam cup from one of the metal canisters.

"I'm guessing it's not the gourmet stuff," Joe said, gesturing to the powdered creamer Bob was now shaking into his cup.

Bob glanced over at Joe as he stirred his coffee with a plastic spoon. "It's not even hot," Bob said.

Joe smiled. "That took a lot of guts what you said back there."

Bob gave his patented shrug. "Thanks." He sipped his coffee. "So it sounds like we share the same delightful storybook."

"Indeed." Joe extended his hand. Bob looked at it as though considering whether to shake it or not.

He eventually took it. "Bob," he said, "though I don't need to tell you that's not my real name."

Joe smiled again. "Call me Not Tom."

Now Bob smiled. "This your first time in group, Not Tom?"

"No. I used to come a little while back, but then I stopped."

Bob sipped his coffee. "Why?"

"Thought I was starting to do good on my own. I'd even found a new outlet, something to *replace* group. It was working great, but lately not so much. So I decided to come back here for a quick pick-me-up, you know?"

Bob sipped more coffee. "What was the outlet?"

"It's a bit complicated. If you feel like grabbing a drink sometime, I could explain it to you."

Bob looked only mildly interested. "Yeah, maybe." He then gestured to Joe's cheek. "Did your setback have anything to do with that?"

Joe laughed. "No, no—I just adopted a cat. We're still getting to know each other."

Bob nodded, finished his coffee in a gulp and then tossed the Styrofoam cup in the trash. "Well, it was nice to meet you, Not Tom. I was hoping I could find an ally here."

Ally, Joe thought. *Perfect.* "I couldn't agree more," he said. "What made you decide to seek help later than sooner?"

"My father died. You'd think it would have been one of the happiest days of my life, but all it ended up doing was bringing back all the old trauma. I don't know why. The nightmares started soon after. My wife made me promise to seek help, so here I am."

"Any kids?" Joe asked.

"A son," Bob said.

And a wife and kid, no less. Bob looked like a fit guy who could handle himself. Joe doubted he could take him by force. But having a wife and kid in the picture? With the right planning, he could take Bob without even breaking a sweat.

"He's another reason I'm here," Bob continued. "The day he was born, I swore I would be the antithesis of my father. And I have been…"

Joe sensed he wanted to say more. He prodded gently. "But…?"

"Lately I've been losing my cool. Giving him shit for the tiniest of things. He came home with a poor grade on his math test, and I crumpled it up and tossed it in his face." Bob paused, his face going from disgust to shame and back to disgust. "Jesus, at that moment I *was* my father."

Joe risked putting a hand on Bob's shoulder. "Hey, that's why you're here, right?"

Bob only nodded, clearly still reliving his atrocious behavior.

"You'll get past it, man," Joe said. "I did."

"Maybe I'll find an outlet like yours."

"My offer stands if you ever want to talk about it outside of group."

"Thanks, man. I just might take you up on it."

Dr. Cole called everyone back to group.

Bob took a seat next to Joe. Joe nearly giggled.

CHAPTER 44

My cell phone rang when I was about to—what else?—step into the shower. It was Morris. I could hear the ambient sounds of traffic behind him.

"What's up?" I answered.

"Call me Bob," he said.

. . .

Morris filled me in on everything that'd happened in group. He claimed our guy went to him like a moth to a flame (his analogy, not mine, of course). Morris even managed to casually confirm the scarring on our guy's right palm when they shook hands. The wound on his cheek required no subterfuge; it was there for everyone to see. Morris said our guy claimed a cat took a swipe at him. Crystal the stripper cat.

. . .

The plan now was simple: wait for our guy to make a move. Morris said our guy had already invited him out for a drink to discuss what he'd termed an "outlet" for all his emotional distress. Pretty gutsy, if you ask me. Not the inviting him out part—we were hoping for something like that—but to declare he had some type of method for dealing with his crazy. I guess it was a testament to how good Morris had been in raising no red flags.

Or perhaps our guy was slowly starting to crack—he'd taken Dr. Cole's bait, after all. All cautious logic would have suggested he'd wait to attend group like he'd initially told Dr. Cole he'd intended to do, but apparently the urge had been too strong, Dr. Cole's on-the-spot clinic on reverse psychology too effective. How Dr. Cole had kept his composure and delivered such an effective spiel after the very real possibility that he was seated across from the serial killer we'd been tracking was the epitome of cool.

And now our guy had taken Morris's bait—with what seemed to be a gaping maw. I gave credit to both Dr. Cole and Morris, but my hopes were with my other consideration: Our guy was beginning to crack. The cautious behavior that had made him so difficult to track from the start was now beginning to lose the race to impulse, as it so often does. In the end, the sick bastards almost always lose to impulse.

The trick was to be there when caution was no longer in the race.

CHAPTER 45

There was another group two nights later. Bob had told Joe he'd be attending but was late in showing. The disappointment Joe felt when group started without Bob rivaled the day at work when the cool guys asked Joe to join them for drinks at lunch and he'd screwed it up.

·   ·   ·

After the first coffee break, Bob finally showed. He looked tired and dejected. Joe all but ran to him at the refreshment table. It was just like it'd been two nights earlier: Bob fixing himself a Styrofoam cup of coffee, Joe sidling up to him, not exactly sure of what he'd say.

"Hey, Bob. Didn't think you'd show tonight."

Bob glanced over his shoulder at Joe. "Hey," was all he said before turning back to preparing his coffee.

Something was definitely wrong.

Joe's concern became a twinge of frustration. Had Bob changed his mind about him? In the two days that passed, had he decided that Joe was not worth talking to, after all?

Had he blown it like he did with the guys from work, goddammit?

"Where you been?" Joe asked. It came out sounding accusatory, and Joe silently scolded himself for it.

"Without sleep," Bob said after sipping his coffee. "I've been without sleep."

"Everything okay?"

"No." He sipped more coffee. There were bags under his eyes.

"Wanna talk about it?"

"The nightmares are worse than ever," Bob said. "This is supposed to be helping, right?" He waved a hand over the room. Some members had remained seated in the circle of chairs; most were outside getting some air. "I feel like all it's doing is making it worse. Bringing out all those skeletons—it's like putting *flesh* on them, you know?"

Joe's frustration vanished. He'd done nothing wrong. The man was simply struggling with his past. More so now. Perfect.

"It gets worse before it gets better," Joe said. "Trust me." He thought about placing a reassuring hand on his shoulder as he'd done the last time but thought better of it. It felt like too much right now.

"I'm not sure I can take much more," Bob said. "I mean, I want to get better, but…"

"But?"

"Last night was a disaster."

Joe's interest was a laser. "What happened last night?"

Bob shook his head. "Never mind."

"*No*," he nearly blurted. "No, Bob, you need to talk about it. Tell me what happened."

Bob stared at his coffee, contemplating.

"Same storybook childhood, remember?" Joe said, putting a hand on Bob's shoulder. It felt right now.

Bob glanced up from his coffee. "I woke up with my hands on my wife's throat."

Joe's interest, previously in exploitation, was now one of true curiosity. "What? Why?"

Bob offered up a helpless shrug. "Sleepwalking, I guess. I was dreaming about my father. Next thing I know, my wife is screaming, and my hands are on her neck." He tossed his cup, still half-full, in the trash. "I still can't wrap my head around it."

"I'm so sorry."

"Yeah…" Bob glanced over at the circle of chairs. "I think I'm gonna go. Take it easy."

"*Wait*," Joe said. "You can't just leave."

"And I can't wait and see whether I end up killing my wife in her fucking sleep. Take it easy, Tom."

"Take me up on my offer!" Joe said. This time he *did* blurt it out. He'd expected more group sessions to pass, more get-to-know-ya chips to accrue before a measure of trust was established between them, affording him greater insurance when he made his move.

But Bob was leaving now, claiming to never return. He couldn't risk losing him. Bob was no consolation prize. Bob was perfect.

"Offer?"

"My outlet. The one that helped *me* cope," Joe said.

"If it was so effective, what are you doing here?"

"Just a quick pick-me-up, remember? My outlet still works. Works *great*."

An agonizing pause.

"Drinks on me," Joe said. "Let's go hit up a bar and I'll tell you everything."

Bob looked at his feet.

"What do you have to lose, Bob?"

Still looking at his feet, Bob began a slow nod. When he glanced back up, he was still nodding, looking like a man at the end of his rope. "Okay," he said. "Okay, what the hell."

Joe's relief weakened his knees. Anticipation fixed it seconds later. Fixed it and then some.

He felt spring-loaded.

CHAPTER 46

Morris called me from his car.

"We're going to a bar," he said.

"What?"

"Yup—following him now."

This seemed odd to me. "I'm surprised he would risk going out in public in the area so soon. Group is one thing, but a bar?"

"He told me it would take about ten minutes to get there. I'm guessing it's more on the outskirts of the city. Maybe he feels it's safer this way."

"Still risky," I said. Then: "So, am I to assume that if you're on your way to a bar, your bluff worked?"

"Yup. Told him I was quitting group. The nightmares, attacking my wife in her sleep, came in looking exhausted and unkempt."

"Big stretch."

He ignored that and said: "I'm gonna try to get him to take me back to his place—or at least someplace more private."

"You make it sound like a date."

"I don't care what it sounds like. He's not going to try anything in a public place."

"So what's the purpose of the drinks?" I looked at the clock on my wall. "And so early? Did group let out earlier than usual?"

"No—but I told him I was leaving early because I couldn't cope anymore. He panicked and offered to take me out for a drink. He promised to tell me about this 'outlet' of his."

"You don't really think he's going to tell you what he actually does, do you?"

"No, of course not. Besides, his word's no good to us."

"Since when is a confession no good?"

"When it's not signed. Attorney's dream about hearsay for their client. Screw that. We need to catch him in the act."

"The act of killing you?"

"That won't happen."

"How many in your cover team?" I asked.

"Six."

Six meant three cars. It didn't seem like enough to me. It was killing me that I couldn't be closer to it all.

"And if you *do* end up going back to his place or somewhere more private?" I said.

"The cover team will be listening, Mags—they'll make the adjustment. Right now it's all about building trust with the guy. We're not expecting him to make a move so soon."

"He went back to group so soon."

"And I give full credit to Dr. Cole's Jedi mind tricks for that. Point is, it would be nice if he made a move tonight, but our hopes aren't too high. If he does try something, we'll be ready."

I sighed into the phone so he could hear it. "Okay...then can you please tell me exactly *what* you have planned for tonight so my blood pressure doesn't make me look like the purple girl in *Willy Wonka*?"

"Violet Beauregarde."

"What?"

"The little girl's name who turned big and purple in *Willy Wonka* was Violet Beauregarde."

"You do realize six agents can hear you right now."

"I'm ashamed of nothing."

"Okay, so tell me—"

"Ah shit, we're here. Hold on, I'm trying to park." A pause and then: "He's coming up to the car, Mags. Call me in twenty minutes. I'll tell him it's my wife and I have to go outside and take it. I'll know more by then anyway."

He hung up.

I looked at the glowing green numbers on my microwave. 8:14.

8:34 felt like weeks from now.

CHAPTER 47

Joe Pierce was wary about going out in public so soon. Group was a minor risk worth taking, but a bar felt major. His picture was out there.

Well, a *sketch* was out there. And really, how many times do you recognize someone from a sketch?

There was the chance of running into someone from the strip club, he supposed, but strip clubs are hardly spots for socializing. You go to look at tits, not your fellow man. Couple that with the fact that he'd bolted from the dimly lit place like his ass was on fire and chances were good the patrons there that day wouldn't be able to place him even in the best of lineups.

That left the stripper and the bouncer. The bouncer had just been stabbed. Chances of him out on the town for drinks so soon after? Zilch.

The stripper? Philadelphia, while not a huge city, was by no means small. And Joe had taken Bob to a place on City Line Avenue, on the outskirts of the city. Applebee's—a family-type restaurant. What kind of stripper would hang out there? Maybe if she had a kid, but it was a long shot.

No, Joe felt good about it all. He would be safe for a little while, and a little while was all he needed. His hope was to eventually get Bob alone. Back at his place would be ideal. Or hell, even Bob's place would do. His first (and wasn't Bob now considered his first? His starting-over first?) had been improvised. Maybe Bob could be improvised too. Perhaps it would be even more special because of it.

. . .

Joe asked for a booth in the far corner of the restaurant. The hostess, a pretty little high-schooler who accommodated Joe's request with practiced chirps and smiles, led them to the far corner of the restaurant where they took their seats, Joe making sure his back was to the masses, just in case.

. . .

"You live close by?" Bob asked.

"Kinda," Joe said. "Why?"

Bob shrugged. "Just wondering why you chose this place."

"You wanna go somewhere else?"

"No—this is fine. Just wondering is all."

A young waitress approached and did a flirtatious welcome-to-Applebee's thing. When it was time to order a drink, Joe insisted Bob choose first. He did and ordered a bottle of Sam Adams.

Joe did the same.

When the waitress asked whether they wanted to put an order in for appetizers, Joe said no thank you; they would just be having a couple of drinks and that was all.

The waitress wasn't flirty after that.

"I don't think she's too happy we're not ordering food," Bob said.

"Are you hungry?" Joe asked. "We can order food if you want."

"No, I'm good."

The waitress brought their beers.

"Cheers," Joe said, raising his bottle.

They clinked necks and took a swig. After the incident at the strip club, Joe would have been okay if he never saw alcohol again. It was days ago, and he *still* wasn't a hundred percent.

How did guys drink every day?

What had his father said to him once, during one of those rare moments when he'd spoken to him without a curl of disgust on his upper lip? *Hair of the dog, kid* (he never spoke his name; it was something his mother and biological father had given him, and a pussy little girl's name at that), he'd said, raising a tumbler of whiskey to his hungover lips. *Aspirin and coffee ain't shit—hair of the dog is the only damn thing that works, kid.*

Did Joe remember a smile after that? He was pretty sure he did. Though in retrospect, Joe knew the smile was a satiating one for what was to come pouring from the tumbler. Still, the message was clear: *Hair of the dog, kid.* To which Joe tacked on his own addendum: *Don't be a pussy, you pathetic mama's boy.*

Joe took a deep pull on the bottle, taking nearly half of it down.

"Thirsty?" Bob said.

Joe burped into his fist. "Needed that," he lied.

Bob gave what amounted to a short courtesy smile. "Listen, man, I'm not one for small talk, especially feeling the way I do now. Any chance we can get right to it?"

Joe frowned as though Bob had asked him a riddle. "It's not really something you *get right to*, Bob."

"I don't follow."

"I'm just saying, I don't think it's something I can sum up in a sentence or two. It might take time."

Bob sipped his beer and looked away. Was he losing interest?

"Something wrong?" Joe asked.

"I thought I made myself clear back at group that time was something I didn't have. I can't keep going on like this."

Joe started an understanding nod. "No, you did; you made it clear. You also said you were at your wits' end, desperate to try anything."

Bob gave a grudging but agreeable nod. "I am," he said. "But I can't keep dredging up all this stuff like we did in group. And if I do, I need to exorcise it quick— right now I feel as if I've got one hell of a demon inside me. *Ten* demons."

He needed something. Bob was losing interest, and he needed something to keep him from leaving.

Joe was now a used-car salesman with a restless mark if there ever was one.

"Let me ask you something, Bob. Who do you blame for your childhood being the way it was?"

Bob squinted. "I'm not sure I follow you."

"Do you blame your father? Your mother? Or do you blame yourself?"

"Why would I blame myself?"

"For being weak."

Bob sat back in his booth. "I *was* weak. I was a child."

"You said in group that you had a son," Joe said.

"That's right."

"...And that lately you've been losing your temper with him."

Bob didn't reply.

Joe kept going. "Do you think maybe you're losing your temper with him because he's a reminder of the way *you* were?"

Bob leaned forward now, elbows resting on the table. "How would you know whether my kid is anything like I was?"

"I *don't* know," Joe said. "That's why I'm asking."

Bob drained the remainder of his beer and slid the empty bottle against the wall, inconspicuous next to the stack of menus and condiments. Joe felt that if Bob wanted another beer, he would have slid the empty bottle to the edge of the table for the waitress to see. The restless mark was close to leaving the dealership, and Joe knew the parallels between his situation and the metaphor shared one undeniable and worrying truth: Once you let them leave, they never come back.

Joe held up both hands and began pumping them in placating apologies. "Listen, man; that came out all wrong. All of it. Thing is, I've never told anyone about my outlet. You're the first. I guess for my first time I did a crappy job trying to explain it."

Bob took his empty bottle from the wall of menus and condiments and placed it on the edge of the table for the waitress to see.

Joe bit back a smile and continued.

"I have an idea; hear me out," he said. "Let's stay here and have another beer, loosen up a bit. After that then we can head back to my place. I can *show* you what I'm talking about, without making a mess of it all by trying to explain it in a crowded restaurant."

"Your place?" Bob said warily.

"Sure, why not? I won't have to weigh my words so carefully for fear of people overhearing."

"Why would you be afraid of people overhearing what you have to say?"

The right words came to Joe instantly, and he was elated.

"Because it's all very personal to me," he said. "I'm sure they wouldn't care one whit if they did overhear, but *I* would. This is for your ears only. Your eyes too."

"You're not some psycho that's going to put my head in the fridge, are you?"

Joe laughed. "I don't need *that* much therapy!"

The waitress approached.

"Can we get another round?" Joe asked.

She left with their order.

"What do you have to lose, Bob?"

"My head," he said with a smile.

Joe laughed again.

The waitress brought their second round of beers, and they clinked necks again, Joe stifling a giggle at the notion of drinking to one's health, as was common.

Bob's cell phone rang. "It's my wife," he said, looking at his phone. "Mind if I take this?"

"Of course not."

Bob left the table and headed outside.

.   .   .

Joe was nearly rocking with anticipation when another waitress approached. "Hi," she said.

"We're good," Joe said. "Another waitress took our order."

"Are you with Agent Morris?"

"Huh?"

"You were sitting with Agent Morris. I work at a coffee shop in West Chester during the day. He and his partner came in to question me a few days ago."

Joe could only stare at her in disbelief. "West Chester?" he managed.

"I know, right? But I'm only here a few nights a week. My father lives in Ardmore, so I just crash at his place when my shift is done."

"West Chester," Joe said again.

"Yeah..." she said, now with a bit of uncertainty. "The West Chester student who was murdered? You *are* with Agent Morris, aren't you?"

"Yes," Joe said.

"Are you with the FBI too?"

"I am, yes."

"Does he have more than one partner?"

"Sometimes. Who was he with when he questioned you?"

"A woman—a redhead. They didn't question me long. They were more interested in questioning Erin, another waitress. She served the guy."

Joe remembered Erin well. The ungrateful bitch who made him look like an ass when he tried to tip her fifty bucks.

"So how are things going?" the waitress asked. "Have you caught the guy yet?"

"No. We were close, but...not anymore."

"Well, I just finished my shift. Will you tell Agent Morris Jen Carr from the coffee shop in West Chester said hello?"

"I sure will."

CHAPTER 48

I called at 8:34 on the dot. I feared voicemail, but Morris answered on the fourth ring. I could hear traffic behind him.

"We're at an Applebee's on City Line Avenue," he said.

"He took you to City Line?"

"Yeah. Maybe he feels paranoid in the city after current events."

"Or maybe he lives close by," I said.

"Well, it looks like I'm about to find out."

"How's that?"

"He invited me back to his place."

"So he actually went for it."

"Yup. He…" Morris trailed off.

"Tim?"

No answer.

"*Tim?*"

"Sorry—some girl was waving at me," he said.

"What girl?"

"Not sure, I couldn't get a good look. Forget it—she was probably waving to someone else."

"What about your cover team?" I asked, getting back to it.

"They'll make the adjustments, Mags. You know the drill."

Yes, I did. An undercover doing a routine getting-to-know-you would have a handful of agents keeping an eye on him or her, as Morris had now. But when getting-to- know-you suddenly took a big leap in the relationship, that protective eye the cover team was keeping needed to become a great big eye in the sky. Literally.

"Air support?" I asked.

"If a serial killer is taking a UC back to his home? Yes, Mags, I would think so."

I wanted to say he didn't have to be a sarcastic dick about it, but I was too concerned for him. And I wanted to let him know. To tell him to be careful and all that. But Morris, like a lot of agents, is superstitious that way. Telling him to be careful is like telling an actor to break a leg before going on stage: Well-meaning, but actually considered bad luck to a thespian.

So instead, I came out with the Pulitzer Prize-winning: "Just catch him."

"That's the plan. Talk soon." He hung up.

CHAPTER 49

Joe Pierce's fingers shook as he hurriedly worked his smartphone, his eyes only leaving the screen to check the restaurant's entrance to make sure Agent Morris hadn't returned yet.

Joe had become a bit of an ace when it came to searching for what he wanted, having followed his own hunt intently over the past year to see whether there had been any breaks in the case he should be aware of.

Everything he'd followed thus far had been local police involvement up and down the East Coast. Never had he come across any FBI involvement, though he wasn't naïve enough to think there wasn't any; his murders had crossed state lines. Still, the Bureau had apparently been doing what it did best: stayed invisible throughout.

Until now.

"Here we go," Joe muttered to himself. His eyes sped over the pics and text of each link like a veteran journalist cranking through roles of microfiche.

A photo of Agent Morris (*Tim* was the bastard's real name) outside the courthouse after testifying in the infamous "Cypher Slayer" case.

A photo of a pretty, no-nonsense-looking redhead (undoubtedly Morris's partner the West Chester coffee girl had just alluded to) outside the same courthouse. "Agent Margaret Allen" it read.

Apparently she was the primary catalyst in apprehending the Cypher Slayer.

Joe kept up a frantic scan, not quite sure what he was looking for now. He'd confirmed that Bob was indeed an FBI agent by the name of Tim Morris. Had confirmed that his partner was a redheaded woman by the name of Margaret Allen.

But so what?

What the hell was he going to do with this information? Wait until Agent Morris got back to the table and triumphantly state that the jig was up, "Bob" old buddy? Or maybe continue with the notion that he was ignorant of Agent Morris's identity and try to get the drop on *him*—an FBI agent, for Christ's sake?

The next link Joe clicked made his mouth drop open.

A photo of Dr. Cole, standing outside the very same courthouse Agent Morris and Agent Allen had been. He'd testified in the very same Cypher Slayer case. And then more of the photo's accompanying text that caused Joe's mouth to drop further still: Dr. Cole's wife had been murdered by the Cypher Slayer.

Joe's head was a raging sea, thoughts drowning and surfacing, yet the survivors were loud and clear:

Dr. Cole's wife was killed by the Cypher Slayer.

Agent Margaret Allen caught the Cypher Slayer.

Agent "Bob" Morris was Agent Margaret Allen's partner.

And then a final, infuriating conclusion:

Dr. Cole had set him up.

"Sorry about that," Agent Morris said as he plopped back down into his booth.

Joe nodded and casually tucked his phone away, blindly clicking off the screen he'd been searching beneath the table. "No problem," he said. "Everything all right at home?"

"Yeah. Things are a little rough right now, the sleepwalking incident and everything. That's why I took the call. Hope I wasn't rude."

"Not at all. Listen, man, I'm gonna have to cancel tonight. Something came up last minute." He brought his phone out from under the table and showed it to Agent Morris before tucking it away again.

Agent Morris frowned. "Everything okay?"

"Got some lady problems of my own," Joe said. "I phoned while you were outside to tell her I couldn't make it over tonight, that you and I were going to hang out instead, and she gave me shit for it. Don't want to be in the doghouse, you know?" He shrugged with a helpless smile.

"That's a shame," Agent Morris said. "I was looking forward to it."

I bet you were, Joe thought. "I'm really sorry, man. What's your schedule like tomorrow? I'm sure I can do it then."

"I'm free," Agent Morris said.

"How about I give you a call?"

"Sounds good." Agent Morris waved over the waitress and asked for a pen. He jotted a number on a napkin and slid it across the table. Joe tucked the napkin into his pocket, wondering whose number it really was.

"Sorry about this," Joe said again.

Agent Morris held up a hand. "No problem at all; I totally understand." He then gestured to their beers. "We can at least finish our beers, can't we?"

If he wanted to arrest you, he'd have done it by now. They don't have anything. Be cool and go with it.

"Of course." Joe smiled, and they clinked necks again.

"Cheers," Agent Morris said.

Joe thought of the notion of toasting to one's health again. It was no longer amusing, but just as ironic.

CHAPTER 50

I was surprised when Morris called me so soon after our last conversation.

"What's wrong?" was my hello.

"It's off," he said. There was traffic in the background again. "He said something came up at the last minute. Girlfriend problems."

"He's got a girlfriend?" I asked.

"Apparently."

"That's odd."

"Bundy had one. Gacy was married. So was Ridgway. I could go on."

"You don't think it's suspicious he cancelled so abruptly?" I asked.

"A little," Morris said. "But he didn't seem in a hurry to get out of there. I asked him if we could finish our beers before he left, and he was okay with it."

"Where is he now?"

"On his way to his girlfriend's, I imagine."

"Is the cover team following?"

"Don't know. I imagine at least one car will follow him for a little bit."

Something still didn't feel right. I wasn't buying the whole girlfriend thing all of a sudden.

"So what now?" I asked.

"He said we could meet up tomorrow. I gave him a number to reach me."

"Well, this turned out to be a big nothing," I said. "Are you just going to call it a night?"

"What would you like me to do, Mags?"

"I don't know." And I didn't. After all the buildup, it felt like the whopping thirty seconds of my first time all over again, minus the backseat.

"I'll swing by," Morris said. "That okay?"

"Sure. What time?"

"Gimme about twenty minutes or so."

CHAPTER 51

Joe Pierce paced throughout his living room, periodically checking his windows to see whether he'd been followed.

He saw nothing.

But then would he? If Agent Morris had been working under-cover, it's not like the FBI would be camped out on his front lawn for all to see.

They could still be there though, watching and waiting in the shadows.

And they would *always* be there, wouldn't they? From now on, they would be watching, waiting for him to...

What? Waiting for him to do what? His suspicions at the restaurant rang just as true now: If they wanted to arrest him, they'd have done so. They had him on assault at the strip club. They could easily bring him in and have the stripper identify him. The bouncer too.

Except they weren't.

They weren't because they wanted him for something bigger. They wanted him for who he really was. They wanted The High Striker. And it was now painfully obvious they were content to wait. Wait until he chose his next victim, catch him red-handed.

Did that mean it was all over? That his work was to come to an end tonight? The very thought was enough to nearly bring him to his knees in a plea to anyone or anything to make it not so. He couldn't lose his life's work. Not now; not when he was just starting over.

Questions swirled. Had he convinced Agent Morris that he wasn't on to him? Yes, he thought so. He hadn't made a mad dash for it when he found out who Agent Morris really was. He'd been damn cool, if he thought so himself. Staying to finish beers with Agent Morris when every fiber of his being was urging him to get the hell out of there. And the girlfriend story seemed believable enough. He'd never had a girlfriend before, but he knew enough about relationships to know that when your lady wanted you home, you went home, right?

And then there was Dr. Cole.

Dr. Cole had set him up. The son of a bitch sat there as cool as can be in group while Agent Morris pretended to be some poor schmuck

(*like you*)

looking for help from his fellow man.

No—not like me. Like I was. Not me now. Like I WAS.

But it's all over now. They're on to you. You can't start over anymore. It's done. Back to who you once were, Jody, you fucking girl.

It's not gonna happen. I won't LET it happen.

You won't, huh? I'm all ears.

Maybe it's time to immortalize The High Striker.

You don't have the balls.

We'll see.

CHAPTER 52

Morris showed up twenty minutes later, just as he said he would. We sat on the sofa and talked with the volume down on the TV, our eyes periodically glancing towards it whenever there was a lull in the conversation.

. . .

"You really buying the whole girlfriend-suddenly-calling thing?" I asked.

He shrugged. "Maybe. Part of the cover team followed him for a bit. He wasn't erratic in his driving. He seemed pretty composed in the restaurant. If he was suspicious, he did a hell of a job concealing it."

I grunted.

Morris splayed his hands. "What do you want me to say, Mags? You're the head cheerleader when it comes to bringing him in for the murders and not the strip club assault. If we want that—and want it to work—we have to wait."

"You think he'll call tomorrow like he said?"

"I don't see why not. 'Bob' is too tantalizing a prospect to discard."

I grunted again. Him Tarzan, me Jane.

"You talk to Dr. Cole?" he asked.

"No, why?"

"We left for a drink in the middle of group. I figured he might be curious if all was well."

I looked at the clock on my wall. "They're probably just wrapping up. Should I call?"

Morris was focused on an infomercial for copper bracelets when he said yes.

.   .   .

I was searching for Dr. Cole's name in my contacts when my phone did its doorbell ding-dong alert, letting me know I had a text.

"Speak of the devil," I said.

Morris turned away from the TV. "That him?"

"Yeah." I read his text. "Group let out. He wants us to swing by if we can."

"Good timing. I don't need a copper bracelet."

I replied: *Be there in 20.*

CHAPTER 53

Group was held in a classroom on the second floor of a high school. Morris led the way, telling me: "Follow Bob." I pointed out that all of the classrooms lining the hallway were dark save for one, and it didn't take a master sleuth to figure out which one Dr. Cole was waiting for us in, thank you.

We entered the one lit classroom.

A click and it was suddenly dark like the others.

Morris said: "What the—?" but got no further. I heard him grunt then drop.

"*Tim?*"

No reply.

Blind movement behind me now. I spun in the darkness, shuffled backwards and tumbled over a body.

The lights came back on. A man was pointing a gun down at me. The body I'd tumbled over was Morris.

"You said twenty minutes," the gun holder said. A lead-weighted leather sap dangled in his nongun hand. "You're late."

I swallowed hard.

"Get up."

I checked Morris first. He was alive but unconscious.

"*Get up.*"

I did.

He took a step towards me, gun raised, barrel now inches from my face.

"You must be Agent Margaret Allen," he said. "The one who caught the Cypher Slayer."

"Yes."

"Think you'll catch *me*?"

He caught me behind the ear with the sap, and I joined Morris on the floor.

CHAPTER 54

It was our own little group therapy session in hell. With our ankles bound together in front, wrists behind the back, torsos tied to our chairs, Dr. Cole, Morris, and I sat facing our therapist—a serial killer holding a gun.

A video camera on a tripod faced us.

"Bad luck," was the first thing our guy said. He was addressing Morris. "When you were outside talking to your"—he made air quotes with his nongun hand—"'wife,' a waitress finishing her shift came over and said you'd questioned her at a coffee house in West Chester." He shook his head, pretending to feel sorry for us. "Bad luck indeed."

I thought about what Morris and I had discussed earlier, about how we often caught the bad guy due to his bad luck. The irony was ever present now, but I refused to appreciate it. The fact that my head ached like a bad hangover helped bury that appreciation. I surely had a concussion. Morris too, I'd imagine.

"You going to kill two FBI agents?" Morris asked.

Our guy smiled. "No—no, tonight you are not FBI agents. Tonight you will be someone else entirely."

"Role-playing? You like doing that, don't you?" Morris snorted. "So sad."

Our guy sucked his teeth, trying to hide his annoyance. "Behave yourself, *Bob*."

"Go fuck yourself, *Tom*."

Our guy took a hateful step towards Morris.

"Tom," Dr. Cole broke in. "Tom, listen to me—"

"Oh, enough with the anonymity bullshit," he said. "It's *Joe*. Joe *Pierce*. Please don't act as if you three masterminds didn't know that already. And if you didn't, it's irrelevant now." He smiled and brandished the gun.

"Okay then, Joe," Dr. Cole said. "Please listen—"

He interrupted Dr. Cole as though he wasn't there, casually pacing before us as he spoke. "I was going to start over...I was going to start over, and it was going to be wonderful, even better than before. But now I can't, can I?" He paused there for a moment, eyes glazing over as though reliving something tragic. He eventually shook his head like a man shaking off a punch. "So I wondered," he continued, "do I stay or do I run? Running is what a coward would do."

"You *are* a coward," Morris said.

"*Tim*," I said.

"No, that's okay, Margaret—do people call you Margaret?"

"Maggie."

"Maggie then. As I was saying, it's okay. Tim's tough-guy persona has only volunteered him to be my father." He smiled at Morris. "Congratulations."

Morris said nothing.

He returned to me. "Maggie? You'll be my mother."

Like Morris, I said nothing.

He faced Dr. Cole now. "Dr. Cole, since your betrayal was especially hurtful, you get to play me—the *old* me."

"Why would playing the old you be such a fitting punishment, Joe?" Dr. Cole asked.

Pierce got right in Dr. Cole's face and began tapping the gun barrel against his forehead. "No, no, no—no mind-melting tonight, Dr. Cole. You are officially off the clock." A final, hard tap of the barrel that made Dr. Cole wince. "Got it?"

Dr. Cole nodded once.

Pierce smiled and headed back towards the video camera.

"What do you have planned, Joe?" I asked. "I imagine this is going to be different than your norm."

He spoke to me while looking through the lens, eerily casual. He could have been a videographer telling his client to hold tight while he checked something. "My norm?" He finished adjusting the lens, stood upright, and said, "What's my norm, Maggie?"

"You kill men," I said. "You exploit their fears, you record it, and then you kill them."

He cocked his head with genuine interest. "You figured that out? The fear part? The recording part?"

"Yes, we did," I said.

"How?" he asked.

I shrugged, the binds pulling uncomfortably against my wrists. "Doing our job."

He nodded as though my vague reply was enough.

"So if this isn't going to be your norm, what *is* it going to be?" Morris asked.

"You don't need to know, Tim—it matters only to me."

This was exactly what I'd been reminding Morris from the start. That we may never get all the reasons, and that if we did get them, they would be a letdown. Rational and irrational share only a word.

Morris wasn't giving up so easily. "Why won't you tell us? We're gonna die, right? What do you have to lose?"

Pierce ignored him and went back to fiddling with the video camera.

Morris went on. "Why are you even filming this one? You going to take your little video to wherever the hell you're planning to run to? Watch it when you're feeling blue?"

"Who said I was running?" He patted the camera as though it were a pet. "This here is for *everyone* to enjoy. You see, Tim, I know that you're right: I can't just kill two FBI agents and hope to disappear. I *will* be found. Brotherhood and all that, I get it. The rulebook would go out the window for me, wouldn't it?"

"Yes, it would," Morris said proudly.

Pierce splayed a hand. "There, you see?"

"So if you're not planning to kill us," I said, "what *are* you planning?"

He retracted his chin as though genuinely surprised. "Oh, I *am* going to kill you, Maggie. I'm going to kill *all* of you. Difference is, when this one's done, I'm going to kill myself too." He tapped two fingers against his chest. "I'm going out like a man."

CHAPTER 55

Joe Pierce stood in front of Morris and produced a bottle of cheap whiskey from a canvas bag. "Time to drink up, Dad." He uncapped the bottle and held it to Morris's mouth.

Ankles bound together but not tied to the chair, Morris kicked both feet into Pierce's shin.

Pierce grimaced in pain and backed up a step. He took a deep breath and exhaled slowly in a bid to regain control. He then moved to the side of Morris's chair, holding the bottle up to Morris's mouth once again.

"Time to drink up, Dad," he said again, his calm requiring blatant effort.

Morris clamped his lips, refusing to drink. Pierce pinched his nose shut. "I can wait," he said.

Morris finally opened his mouth to breathe, and Pierce jammed the neck of the bottle in, clanking teeth. Morris coughed wildly as the whiskey went down, continuing long after Pierce took the bottle away.

He moved to Dr. Cole next. "Hello, Jody," he said to Dr. Cole. "Are you ready?"

Jody?

"I'm not you, Joe," Dr. Cole said. "None of them were."

"*Fucking coward!*" Morris blurted after coughing up the last of the whiskey.

"Tim, shut up!" I yelled.

"No, that's okay, Mom," he said to me. "He's just being Dad."

Jesus, Morris was giving the sick bastard exactly what he wanted.

He left Dr. Cole and approached me again, pulled something from the canvas bag, and held it up in front of my face. It was a silver lion the size of a large walnut.

"I need you to give this to Jody, Mom," he said to me. "Can you do that?"

The switching from Joe to Jody puzzled me. "To *Jody*?" I said.

"Yes," he said. "*I* am Joe. *That*"—he pointed to Dr. Cole—"is Jody. Got it?"

I nodded.

He held the silver lion in front of my face again. "So can you give this to Jody, Mom?"

"To protect him?" I asked. "Give him courage for what's to come?"

He paused his act, looking suddenly shaken, as if someone from the audience had jeered, causing him to fumble his lines.

"Yes," he eventually said. "Tell him to hold it tight, to never let go no matter what."

"Of course I will," I said.

Again he paused, looking a little rattled at my willingness to comply.

"How can I though?" I said, flipping my chin over my shoulder, gesturing towards my binds behind my back.

"Give me permission to do it," he said.

"But then it won't be the same."

"Just do it," he insisted.

"Please give it to Jody," I said. "To give him the courage to withstand his father."

This time he pulled away from me, turning his back in frustration. *I* was playing director, not clueless participant, and it was getting to him. I needed to tread carefully, though; his weapons were far more immediate than mine. Fortunately (or unfortunately?), I did not have to create anything, only draw from my own past.

He spun back to us and quickly approached Dr. Cole as though his immediate actions might mute the job I was doing inside his head. He stood behind Dr. Cole and placed the silver lion in his hand. Dr. Cole did not resist.

"Good," he said. "Good."

He returned to face all three of us. "How you doing over there, Dad? Want another?"

Morris said nothing, now aware of how his temper was playing into it all.

"Dad?"

Morris only drilled him back with his eyes, refusing to speak.

"I'll take that as a yes."

He approached Morris and repeated the same procedure: fingers clamping the nose tight until Morris had no choice but to gasp and swallow and choke.

"Good," he said again. "Atta boy, Dad."

"You hate your father," I said.

He shot me a glance. "I hate *you.*"

"*Me?*"

"You coddled me. It's your fault I am the way I am."

Dr. Cole said: "There's nothing wrong with the way you are, Joe—"

"*SHUT UP!*" Pierce spun and punched Dr. Cole on the side of the face, rocking him in his chair. The silver lion fell from his hand and clattered to the floor. Pierce snatched it back up and pressed it hard into Dr. Cole's palm, making him form another fist over the lion. Through clenched teeth, he then hissed: "I swear to God, Dr. Cole, if you don't hold on to that, this will be the longest night of your fucking life, got it?"

Dr. Cole gave a weak nod.

"Got it...*Jody?*"

A stronger nod.

Pierce slapped him. "*Got it, Jody?*" He slapped him again. "*Got it, Jody!?*" A punch now, snapping Dr. Cole's head back. "*GOT IT,*

JODY!?" A second punch followed by two more slaps, Dr. Cole silently taking them despite his pain.

"*Stop!*" I yelled.

Pierce ignored me and moved behind Dr. Cole's chair. Gripped his hair and jerked his head skyward. "Jody's a girl's name," he seethed. "A sissy fucking *girl's* name." He spat down on Dr. Cole's bloodied face before releasing the grip on his scalp and circling the chair to face him again. He spat on him once more, saliva and blood soon coming together in a slow drip on the point of Dr. Cole's chin.

"Look at you…for the love of Christ, *look at you.*" He gripped Dr. Cole by the neck. "You gonna cry? You gonna cry, you little pussy? Huh? Gonna go cry to Mommy, you pathetic pussy mama's boy?" He let go of Dr. Cole's throat and slapped him again. "Come on, cry." Slapped him again. "*Cry!*" Slap. "*Cry, you little pussy!*" Slap. "*Cry!!!*"

"*STOP!*" Morris yelled.

Crazily enough, Pierce did. Panting, he glanced over at Morris with wild eyes as though woken from the throes of a nightmare.

"I thought *I* was playing your father," Morris said.

Still panting, Pierce only continued to stare at Morris with those wild eyes.

Again, Morris said: "I thought *I* was playing your father."

Pierce started nodding, slow at first, and then quicker, more demonstrative with each bob of the head. "You're right…you're goddamn right…" He stood in front of Morris. "Give me permission."

"Huh?"

"Give me permission to be my father."

"No."

"Come on, Tim, your partner played along. Give me permission."

"No way."

Pierce clenched his jaw and enunciated slowly through gritted teeth. "*Give me permission to be my father.*"

"If you become your father, does that mean I get to be you?" Morris said. "Hey, look at me! I'm a pathetic piece of shit who copes with his bad childhood by torturing and killing innocent people! *Boo! Hoo! Hoo!* Life is so unfair!"

Pierce spun, snatched up his gun, spun back and rammed the barrel into Morris's mouth. "*Want another, Dad!? Huh? Want another!???*" Morris gagged on the barrel as Pierce drove it in deeper. "*Give me permission!!!*"

"*STOP IT!*" I screamed.

Gun still in Morris's mouth, Pierce whipped his head towards me. "What are *you* gonna do, Mom? *Huh?* You gonna save *him* like you saved *me?*"

He ripped the gun from Morris's mouth and then maneuvered his way behind Dr. Cole. Took the silver lion from Dr. Cole's fist and brought it over to me, thrusting it in my face.

"*This!? This* is how you help me!?" He threw the lion at me.

I flinched and turned my head away. Locked eyes with Morris. He was no longer coughing from the gun barrel, but working furiously on the binds behind his back...and making progress, his determined gaze speaking to me as he worked: *Keep him busy, Mags.*

I instantly brought my head back around and locked eyes with Pierce.

"I'm sorry she couldn't help you more, Joe," I said. "She was afraid too."

He got in my face. "You were weak. You were weak, and you made *me* weak."

I played along. "I was scared too, but I loved you and helped you the only way I was capable."

He grabbed my throat with one hand and pressed the gun to my head with the other. "*I hate you! I fucking HATE YOU!*"

"I'm sorry...I am so, *so* sorry..."

He jerked away from me, shut his eyes tight and began banging the side of his head with his nongun hand. "*I HATE YOU I HATE YOU I HATE YOU I HATE YOU I HATE YOU!!!*"

"Who are you talking to, Joe?" I asked.

He snapped from his daze, looked at me with a self-loathing even my own mirror had never shown me in my darkest hours, and lunged for me.

I leaned back and whipped both bound feet up and into Pierce. Morris's legs are long; when he'd tried it, he caught Pierce in the shin.

Mine are short; I caught him smack in the balls.

Pierce bucked forward in pain, his face coming within inches of mine. I used this and snapped my head forward with everything I had, catching him in the face with a headbutt that shot him back on his ass, gun flying from his hands and skidding across the classroom floor.

I rocked backwards once and then forward with a powerful lunge, finding my feet, chair still attached to my back, hands still bound to it.

I could hear Morris screaming, telling me to hold on.

Pierce was scrambling to all fours, frantic eyes all over in search of the gun.

We spotted it simultaneously, exchanged a quick, desperate glance, then went for it, him diving from all fours, me with my ankles bound and a damned chair on my back.

He arrived first, snatching the gun in his hand. I arrived a split second after, hopping like a crazed rabbit and bringing one of the chair legs down onto his hand, crushing it, causing him to cry out, abandon the gun, and roll away.

Seated now in the chair, I kicked the gun farther away with both feet, felt his good hand latch onto my scalp from behind a second after, jerking me and the chair backwards, only to stop and wrap his forearm around my throat and begin to squeeze.

Pierce frothed out incoherent rantings as he squeezed tighter and tighter. My vision became a tunnel, the exit of light in the distance narrowing and slipping further and further away as unconsciousness closed in.

> *Stop fighting and let go.*
> *No.*
> *Let go and I promise you'll die this time.*
> *No.*
> *You'll get to see Christopher...*
> *Not yet.*

See Mike...
Not yet.
Just let go...
No...
...
...

Bursts of gunfire echoing in the tunnel. The exit of light in the distance growing suddenly larger, coming closer.

A brief silence. I could feel movement around me, could feel movement *on* me, someone jostling me.

"*Come on, Maggie...*"

The exit of light growing larger still, faster as I'm propelled towards it.

"*Come on, Maggie!*"

A blast of light now, all around me. I shut my eyes against it and rolled onto my side.

"Maggie...oh thank God." Morris's voice, laden with relief.

I rolled back towards his voice, shielding the light above with my hand. "I hate when you call me Maggie."

He chuckled, on the verge of tears. "Mags..."

"Better." I sat up, bracing myself with one arm.

The room was spinning. I spotted the gun by Morris's side and then caught his eye. He flicked his chin towards the corner of the room where Joe Pierce lay dead, blood pooling beneath his torso, eyes unblinking on the powerful classroom lights above.

I wondered whether he was in the tunnel before he went. I wondered whether he fought for the exit of light or welcomed the black.

.   .   .

While we were waiting for help to arrive, Dr. Cole showed me his palm, the damage the silver lion had done. I asked him why he kept squeezing through it all, why he didn't just hold the lion slack in his hand; Pierce would have never known.

He admitted to squeezing in hopes that it would all go away.

234

CHAPTER 56

A week later and Dr. Cole had Morris and me over for dinner.

The subject of Jody Pierce, aka "The Philly Phantom" (the shameless media wasted no time in replacing "The High Striker" with something spookier and easier to comprehend for the masses), was unavoidable. We'd made a valiant effort to enjoy our evening without reliving the events we'd endured, but it soon became hard to ignore the fact that the only reason we were able to appreciate the evening was *because* of the events we'd endured.

*   *   *

At first, we gave the difficult stuff the Band-Aid treatment, ripping it off quickly so as not to prolong its memory.

Dr. Cole certainly needed no reminder; he was still marked up pretty good from where Pierce had beaten the crap out of him.

Morris was missing a tooth. Apparently Pierce had knocked it clean out while chipping two others when he jammed the barrel of the gun into his mouth.

Whereas Dr. Cole wore his lumps quietly, Morris was not as keen to do so, constantly reminding me that the freaky senses I often experienced while using high doses of the drug were dearly missed towards the end of our investigation and would have saved us all a lot of work *and* pain, had they decided to show.

I wanted to remind him (for the umpteenth time) that I had no control in how or when the damn drug worked, or that perhaps the side effects had faded with continued use as I'd suggested before.

Dr. Cole was also quick to side with me on this, but even more adamant in pointing out his initial assertion weeks ago that I was a more than capable enough investigator without pharmaceutical help.

I didn't argue and simply stated what I'd said from day one: I was capable, but the drug sure as hell expedited things. And while the drug's ability to heighten my senses had lost steam towards the end for any number of reasons, it certainly did a nice job of pointing us in the right direction from the start.

Sure, my being able to point Jody Pierce out in a crowd on day one would have been nice, but we knew that was never going to happen. Morris had just needed something, *anything* to go on at the time, and the drug had done exactly that, finding us a detour around that blocked road every agent experiences at one point or another in their career.

But still, it was hard to argue with Morris, whether he was just teasing at this point or not (and he probably was). Had the drug carried its impact during the entire course of the investigation, who knows how much sooner we might have found Jody Pierce and saved ourselves the pain and grief we'd endured? But in my opinion, that was the unforgivingly chaotic and never tidy thing called life. The end. At least we ended up alive, and the crazy bastard dead.

．　　．　　．

As for me, I was ironically the least scathed, even though I'd come the closest to death among all three of us. Then again, I wasn't counting mental scars…and I didn't need to. Crazy as it seems, nearly dying gave me perspective.

I told Dr. Cole this during drinks after dinner, glasses raised at the table, ready to take the first sip of our rightfully deserved medicine.

"You know what today is, Dr. Cole?" I said.

He gave that little smile of his. "No, Maggie. What?"

"It's *Irony Appreciation Day* again."

"How's that?"

"I survived this ordeal because I wanted to live."

Morris frowned at both of us. "How is that ironic?"

Dr. Cole looked at me with that little smile when he answered Morris. "Trust us; it makes sense."

CHAPTER 57

I dreamt hard that night.

I'm at the Little League baseball field Morris and I had visited in West Chester. I'm the boy crying in his mother's arms. My father comes over to grab me, but Morris grabs him first, flinging him backwards onto his butt where he hits the dry infield, kicking up a cloud of dust. My father's image then dissolves with the cloud as it settles into the earth, taking my fear of him with it. My mother whispers in my ear that I'm safe now. She then gestures with her chin towards the outfield, and I see Christopher in uniform, healthy, waiting for play to resume. He smiles and waves to me. I glance up at the bleachers, and Mike is there. He smiles and waves to me too. I look back at the settled cloud of dust, and my father is still gone. I look up at my mother and smile, and she smiles back with a desperate love in her eyes, squeezing me tight.

.　　.　　.

I woke and found the music box I'd purchased sitting on my night table.

I knew it was broken, but I opened it anyway.

It worked.

I listened to "All the Pretty Little Horses" over and over, silently thanking my mother for all she was able to do for me, despite her fear.

I squeezed the box tight and it dug into my palm, yet it didn't hurt. It was oddly comforting.

I wasn't sure whether I was still dreaming, and I didn't care—it was the best I'd felt in a long time.

ACKNOWLEDGMENTS

A huge thanks to my uncle, Tom Menapace, for his insight into FBI procedure and the like. A retired Special Agent with 33 years of service to the FBI, Tom was part of the original NYPD-FBI Joint Terrorism Task Force, has received numerous commendations for individual cases, and was twice recognized for sustained outstanding performance (MVP) in the terrorism field. The endless phone calls and emails of mine this poor man had to endure… Tack on one more commendation for outstanding patience. If you see any errors other than liberties for the sake of fiction, they are mine.

Thanks again, Uncle Tom.

ABOUT THE AUTHOR

A native of the Philadelphia area, Jeff Menapace has published multiple works in both fiction and non-fiction. In 2011 he was the recipient of the Red Adept Reviews Indie Award for Horror.

Jeff's debut novel *Bad Games* was a #1 Kindle bestseller that spawned three acclaimed sequels, and now the first three books in the series have been optioned for feature films and translated for foreign audiences.

His other novels, along with his award-winning short works, have also received international acclaim and are eagerly waiting to give you plenty of sleepless nights.

Free time for Jeff is spent watching horror movies, The Three Stooges, and mixed martial arts. He loves steak and more steak, thinks the original 1974 *Texas Chainsaw Massacre* is the greatest movie ever, wants to pet a lion someday, and hates spiders.

He currently lives in Pennsylvania with his wife Kelly and their cats Sammy and Bear.

Jeff loves to hear from his readers. Please feel free to contact him, and be sure to visit his website to sign up for his FREE news-letter (no spam, not ever) where you will receive updates and sneak peeks on all future works along with the occasional free goodie!

CONNECT WITH JEFF ON SOCIAL MEDIA:

http://www.facebook.com/JeffMenapace.writer

http://twitter.com/JeffMenapace

https://www.linkedin.com/in/JeffMenapace

https://www.goodreads.com/JeffMenapace

https://www.instagram.com/JeffMenapace

OTHER WORKS BY
JEFF MENAPACE

Please visit Jeff's Amazon Author Page or his website for a
complete list of all available works!

http://www.amazon.com/Jeff-Menapace/e/B004R09M0S

www.jeffmenapace.com

AUTHOR'S NOTE

Thank you so much for taking the time to read *Side Effects*. I hope you enjoyed reading the adventures of Maggie and Morris as much as I did writing them. Who will they be hunting next? And will Maggie be doing it with or without the help of the drug? Hmmm...

Every single reader is important to me. Whenever I'm asked what my writing goals are, my number one answer, without pause, is to entertain. I want you to have fun reading what I write. I want to make your heart race. I want you to get paper cuts (or Kindle thumb?) from turning the pages so fast. Again—I want to entertain you.

If I succeeded in doing that, I would be very grateful if you took a few minutes to write a review on Amazon for *Side Effects*. Good reviews can be very helpful, and I absolutely love to read the various insights from satisfied readers.

Thank you so very much, my friends. Until next time...

Jeff

47194631R00151

Made in the USA
Middletown, DE
05 June 2019